Esther Bligh

Esther Bligh

by

Diana Powell

www.hhousebooks.com

Paperback ISBN: 978-1-910688-65-6
Kindle: 978-1-910688-66-3

Cover design by Jo Dalton: Studio 59

Typeset by Polgarus Studio

Published in the USA and UK

Holland House Books
Holland House
47 Greenham Road
Newbury, Berkshire RG14 7HY
United Kingdom

www.hhousebooks.com

For my four Davids – always

It is dark again. I prefer the darkness now. Perhaps I always have.

'Night-bird', he called her, 'Esther, my little nightingale.'

Outside is wiped away.

Outside, with its treacherous sunlight, its mocking colour, the insinuating rumour of the sea; outside, where the crones gather in the square, whispering behind their claws, and the gargoyle children grimace and gibber.

What do they know? What *can* they know? Nothing. They have no proof. There *is* no proof. Is there?

I can draw the curtains, shutting it – them – out. Now I am safe inside and inside is all that matters. I can build up the fire, eat my meal, then retreat to bed.

Not that *bed; she doesn't sleep in* that *bed,* that *room, any more.*

Soon I will be lying there, and will pull the blankets higher, and the pillow lower

Not that *pillow, she burned that one; she remembers the feathers melting inwards, crying weakly, as if she were killing the birds themselves.*

until I am comfortable and snug. I will be safe. I am safe in here. (Am I safe? Truly safe?)

Tomorrow, I do not have to go out, or the next day, or the next. Enough food for a week has been delivered to my door, so I can stay in bed as long as I like, away from the windows, away from the light, away from them all.

And in the morning, when another letter comes, I will put it on the fire straight away, burn it,

just as she did to that pillow, and the sheets, the blankets, and her gloves, and...

as I should have done with the first one. I should never have read it. I should never have allowed the words to reach me, to follow me inside. Let them stay in the darkness out there.

From the moment the driver left her, the village has been cowled in gloom, cloud seeping down the mountains to meet mist rising off the sea; rain, rain and more rain. Now it is dark again, so she pulls the curtains. Once upon a time, Grace craved the dark, seeking it out in the furthest crannies of her old home, delving deep under the bedclothes, leaving lights and fires unlit; she wore black and buried herself in the dark house.

When she came out, a red hat, topped with a peacock's multi-coloured feathers sat proudly on her head, while its shimmering eye cast a disdainful look on the dark plumage beneath – her plain grey dress. For grey was wrong – too dull. Still, it was all she had, until she found yellow and scarlet and emerald green, pushed to the back of the ancient armoire in the bedroom not opened in twenty years. A purple dress, shawls, scarves in rainbow hues. Clothes from her trousseau, bought long ago, but fitting her still. She smiled at that.

People noticed her then as she strutted down streets she had forgotten, to shops she did not recognise. 'Where has she come from?' perhaps they said. But she had always been there. Just locked away.

'I am Grace. I was grieving for my husband, John, lost in the mud and the gas,' she might say, if they asked. But they kept their words for behind cupped hands, offering mocking shrugs and scornful laughs instead.

But she didn't care. She was happy. John had come back. Not to have and to hold, as he once said, but to talk to her, and listen, putting different words in her head, besides her own; a companion, a friend. There were others voices, too, some she had known, some she had not, but knew them now – old, young; from different ages or distant lands. A few were strange and fearful, at first, gruff and growling. Others, always pleasing to her ear, like the most familiar, who trilled like a nightingale. So, now, she was no longer alone. There was no need for wailing, rending of garments, and despair of the soul any more; no need for the dark, and the black, and burying herself away. She was alive again, just as they were.

A murmur of air. A sigh – *her* sigh. Or—

– Light the fire; turn on the lights, make some tea.

– But nothing I do warms the place, or brightens it. Look at me, wearing my coat indoors, look at these cheerless rooms.

As soon as she stepped through the door, fingers of ice reached around her, and held her tight. But it was the same outside: the cold and rain; the buildings of grey stone topped with black slate, blurring back into the mountains; the people, with their dark countenances, and strange language.

– What kind of place have I come to? You told me it was beautiful. 'A picture post-card', you said.

– But you said it, too. That was how you remembered it.

Two days she and John had spent here. Their honeymoon, where she had first worn the rainbow clothes and been happy.

– It will be different when the spring comes, and the summer. That's what they tell you, anyway.

– The difference between summer and winter, a half circle of the earth around the sun. Is that all it is? Perhaps I should have waited; perhaps this was a foolish time to move. And the house – you said… and the people, you told me they were friendly. And…

– Shhh, now! Ssshh!

'Whore.

...bitch

Slut.'

The words follow me inside the bed now, creeping through the floor-boards, climbing through the gap between the clasped shutters, worming their way beneath the quilt, the sheet, the pillow pulled low, to where I lie curled tightly like the centre of a moon snail.

'Look, see,' he told her, scooping something from the sand. A shell. Nothing more. She had thought it must be treasure, a ruby, at least. 'A moon snail, or necklace shell. See the perfect spiral. So beautiful... like you.'

Sometimes, they burrow deeper, and reach inside me – dreams where disembodied faces pass in front of me, their twisted mouths spitting their bile. 'SSSssslut!' quick and slippery; or, through smacking lips, BB/ChCh 'Bitttchh...chch'. Or night-terrors when words unhook themselves from the page one by one, the letters drifting loose, H A G S P A W N, separating into black tendrils that sssstretch longer and longer, and swarm around me, snaking around my throat, tighter and tighter, until I can no longer breathe.

Dreams, or not dreams. It is the same when I am awake. There is no escape.

I knew the words long ago. From... before. And later, from the streets of London, the soldiers calling at me, where I stood in Piccadilly; laughing – those who did not want me.

And then he came, older, uglier than most, with his wrung-out face, and threads of salt-and-pepper hair. Still, he took my hand, and led me away.

'Same as the others,' I thought. 'He'll take me to a cheap room, or a filthy alleyway.'

But no. He took me to the nearest Lyons, where I could be warm. He bought me food and drink, because I looked so thin. He talked. About the war. About his home.

'Look,' he said, pulling a post-card from his notebook.

A quiet sea lapping towards the tall, elegant houses, with gentle mountains rising behind. 'In Wales,' he said. 'The most wonderful place.'

'And this – where I live.' A house not joined to others, windows on either side of the door; trees, a lawn – things I hardly knew. 'Cross the road, and there is the sand, the sea. Heaven. Bliss!'

'Why's he gabbing?' I wondered. Most of the bastards said nothing, except to make it clear who I was and what they wanted of me. That I was not the same as the strawberries-and-cream girlfriends they had left behind, or their saintly mothers, their rose-tinted sisters. 'Get on with it,' I thought. There was no need for conversation like this. Still, I talked back, in my sweetest voice, as it seemed to please him.

'... like the song of the nightingale,' he told her. 'That is what I will call you. My night-bird.'

And then, stranger still, could I meet him tomorrow? For lunch, perhaps, as if I were the kind of woman who dined at the Criterion at midday, between her morning and afternoon tea. And I said 'yes'. Why not? A free meal, in a warm place. And there was money there, I knew, with the house so grand, the way he talked. A gentleman. Perhaps something might come of it.

'Whore.' Sometimes the word would snigger after me, as I walked arm in arm with him down Oxford Street. A soldier

I had serviced? A jealous 'friend'? There were plenty of those.

'Take no notice,' he would say. 'They don't know you,' he would say, as I raised my eyes to his, and clutched him tighter.

'I know you, Esther, I know your true self. You are better than you think you are.' She laughed. 'Let me tell you what I did,' she said, and whispered in his ear.

'It will be different when we are married,' he said. 'It will be different when you are Mrs. Edmund Bligh, when we are in Wales – the people are so friendly there. You will be welcomed and respected. You will love it!'

This is what had come of it.

A rushed ceremony in a back-street office. They were used to it then, with the soldiers and their floozies, wanting their weddings before France, the trenches, death. Witnesses pulled off the streets. It was easy. But there was to be no death, he was sure. 'The war is all but over. This is no more than information-gathering. I'll be back before you know it, and then I'll take you home.' Home. The word always wrapped in smarming breath. So special, so meaningful, as if that were how all homes were. As if he had no knowledge of rats grinning at you from corners, black mildew serving as patterned wallpaper, the stench of week-old stew mingled with stale piss.

'Still, I'll make provision, just in case.' Another office, a solicitor's, this time; another two witnesses. And then a night in a hotel room. *I* made sure of that. I needed to make sure of that.

Then he was gone, to return even sooner than expected, coming back even less of a man than before, twisted and torn here, there and everywhere, in body, mind and spirit.

'Home,' he mouthed, that same word again, as if it would

make everything right, when all was wrong already.

There had been no need. The bleeding had come the day after he had left for France. The bleeding I had looked to buy with the money he'd given me for 'a new coat to keep you warm/New shoes, because those are worn/New lodgings, while I am gone, where there is no damp, no mice.' But the money hadn't bought what I wanted from it. The expensive ways turned out to be no better than the ones I had always used, and had been trying for weeks. I knew them all, and they all failed me. And so I had said 'yes' to the marriage.

I had said 'yes' to a broken man. I'd said 'in sickness and in health, till death us do part, as long as we both shall live.' 'Yes' to a place on the other side of the country, where I would live with a fool.

I had said 'yes' to here.

Ssshh… Hushhh. Shusshh… Most of the voices are quiet today. This is how they can be – no more than a distant humming, the buzzing of a wasp trapped in a honey-jar. Today, it is as if a group of women has gathered in the attic above her, to put their heads together, their hands in front of their mouths, and whisper. Not unlike the women she has seen gathered in the Square, not unlike the women in the old place, until they could no longer stop their words escaping and flying towards her.

'Mad,' they said.

'Poor soul!' – those kinder ones.

Soon, they had dug out the tale.

'John Marlowe's widow, Grace…'

'I thought she was dead…'

'Crazy old bat…'

Not so old, she thought: middle-aged, maybe, but still young enough to have a life now John was back, together with all her other companions; now that she knew there was an after-life, or some other dimension, where all could live happily ever after. If only she had known it sooner, if only they had come to her sooner.

But this is how they were – a kind of coming-and-going motley crew, mainly women, except for John, of course. And the old Red Indian chief who appeared now and then.

When the new war came, they grew quiet for a while, cowed by a conflict that was not supposed to happen. She was afraid, then, that they had gone for good. Perhaps they were needed elsewhere. Or what if the connection between them was lost amongst the falling bombs, the guns firing and the aircraft screeching? There had been talk amongst the crowd who gathered in the shelters of radar, and other strange devices… perhaps these things 'interfered'?

John was quiet, too, then. She understood why. How hard it must be to see all this death, again, when he had fought to put an end to it! Surely even a spirit would be silenced by such injustice.

Still, there was one voice that stayed with her – a sweet, sympathetic voice. A woman who understood her past pain. She had also lost her husband, in the last war, she said; she, too, had shut herself away.

– A mistake. I see it now.

– I should have left there, moved away.

– A change of scenery is good.

– A change is as good as a rest.

– A new start, and all that.

I should have.

I could have.

You could…

You should…

Yes.

Why not? Other people were leaving the cities for places where they might be safe from the war. But where to? And then she remembered.

Or she thinks she remembered. What she knows is that she came across a post-card as she was clearing out the wardrobe. Strange, she hadn't noticed it before, when it seemed so obvious, lying there, in full view. Strange, too, that there was no dust on it, when everything around it was grimed with the years of neglect. But she was used to 'strange' by then.

She picked up the card, and looked at it closely. Golden sand, and bright blue sea. A row of houses stood just beyond the beach, with green hills reaching to a cloudless sky. The colours were harsh, and of a different time. Still, despite this strangeness, she knew at once where it was.

Where it was was *here.*

– Go out. Put on the peacock hat, and the brightly coloured clothes; walk across the road, to look at the sea. Then carry on along the front, to the post-office/shop, and buy a loaf of bread; talk to the post-mistress.

She has done this a few times now – only a few, the weather has been so unkind, there has been no pleasure in it, with sea murk so thick the view stays invisible. And she has never been one for idle chatter, but likes to be polite. Besides, she is determined to be different here, to start afresh and make new friends.

– Smile at all the people you meet, if they can be seen through the gloom, and they will smile back, this time, surely, and say 'hello' – or 'boar ray da', if that is what they say. Something like that.

– Go out. The weather is better, or not so bad. The rain is no more than a constant drizzle, the wind no more than a fresh breeze, the cold no more than a steady chill.

– I am going out.

– Is it wise… The weather? Better to stay in, perhaps.

– I cannot stay in another day. I cannot go back to how it was before. I—

– But it would be foolish to catch a cold. Easily done in this dampness, inside and out.

It is true, the corners of the house are mottled grey; strips of wallpaper sink idly to the floor, her breath mists in front of her. The windows are misted, too, inside and out, blocking the light and the view to the sea. The place smells – of damp, and mildew and rot… and something else that Grace cannot identify. Nothing has changed here in years.

The dark panelling, the heavy furnishings all add to the gloom. The fires she lights sputter and sag; she cannot get them going. The range falters on vaguely most of the time, but the living room hearth is full of charred sticks, curled paper, the relics of her forlorn attempts.

'A mistake, perhaps, in coming here?' John, now. She has noticed this, how John will interrupt the other, as if… what?

– As if he is jealous, perhaps?

– No, it is not that, surely. As if…

'But you said. You told me we would come back.'

They had sat on the wall, looking out at the sea. She can see the place, if she strains forward from the dining-room window. A sheltered spot, closer to the cliffs. 'Do you have to go?' she whispered, knowing, of course, that he did. She had known it from the moment she first met him, proud in his uniform. A chance meeting, outside the bank Daddy had once managed. Love at first sight for both of them, they agreed later. Before she knew it, they were married. There was just time for a honeymoon. Here.

'We'll come back,' he said. 'Once the war is over, for longer. Perhaps, even, one day, we could live here. Buy one of the houses on the front, raise a family.'

She had looked back to the houses they had walked past. Tall, elegant houses, built in Victoria's time for the retired sea-captains, perhaps. Each had a small, leafy garden – a perfect place to sit and watch the sea. A perfect place for children to play. She doesn't know if she saw this one. Perhaps the trees hadn't been cut then. Perhaps she had thought it too grand to imagine they could live here. Soon after, they went back to the guest house and made love again. The first of their family began there, she was sure.

She was right. There was a baby inside her, for a few

weeks at least. Until the telegram arrived, telling her John was missing, presumed dead, and the grief that overwhelmed her took the child away from her, too.

'I'm sorry.'

– Don't cry. Finish with crying.

Crying killed the baby – the wracking of her body, day after day, week after week, tearing insides out, until the bleeding began, until it was certain. Until no more than a husk remained, shrouded in black, camouflaged in the deepest corners of his bequeathed house. Refusing entry to friends and family, the few that existed. A cousin of Daddy's, not seen since his funeral, when she was five years old; Julia, who had been with her in St. Mary's; one or two others she can hardly remember. She had never had a large social circle, preferring to stay at home with Mother. Soon, they stopped coming, leaving her to year after year after year, locked in silence.

'I didn't know you could hear silence. The way it followed me around the house, which gave me nothing. No creaking floorboards, no clanging pipes, no whistling draughts. And I would lie in bed, listening, thinking to hear my heart, if nothing else, and when there was still nothing, I would think 'Good, I am dead'.'

'Sssss, wwwhirrr, GGGrace. Hello.'

That is how it started, she remembers. Wisps of sound, then a word or two, her name, a greeting.

'Grace, Grace. Listen to me, Grace. Shhh, ssss, here. No, I am here. Me, meee, meeee…'

Different voices clamouring, female, a man? A child, maybe? A muddled cacophony, then growing clearer.

'We are all here.'

'I laughed then.' It was a strangled sound, an action her mouth, her throat, her breath – whatever was needed to make laughter – were so unused to, she choked almost.

'Then I tried again, because I had heard you amongst them! And I was so happy, I wasn't alone any more. And I will be happier still, here, soon. As soon as the weather changes, and I settle. As soon as I get this place sorted, and now, with the war ending, the place will pick up again, and I will open my little guest house…'

This was her plan. Or she thinks it was hers. It came to her, soon after she found the post-card. 'I made enquiries, and discovered that one of the houses on the front was for sale. Right at the end, near the cliffs. The biggest, the best, just requiring a little work. It had been for sale for years, apparently, waiting for me. There was no need for me to view it. The whole village had been wonderful, as I remembered – not a poor property anywhere.'

'Perfect!' the sweet voice dripped honey in her ears.

'Hopeless,' someone else offered. 'You'll never sell while they are still fighting.' But it turned out she didn't have to. There was money she hadn't known about, in an account she had never paid attention to. John was wealthier than she imagined. It was something she had never asked about in their short time together. Loving him was all that mattered. Soon the purchase was all arranged. Soon, somehow, she was here. All she needed now was the weather.

– I will go out. She sighs, watching the rain dashing along the front chased by the wind.

– You will get drenched.

– Better to stay in.

– Better…

– Yes, better, perhaps.

Whorebitchslut… Liar.

… 'Liar!' A tame word, a word I can dismiss easily enough. Who doesn't lie?

'LIAR!' A word from childhood, childish, between sisters, to go with 'fibber!' 'I'll tell! Do that again, an' I'll tell on you. You little bitch.'

'Tell, and nobody'll believe you.'

'If you tell, I'll punish you more.' Not my sister, not then.

Yes, everyone lies. Even *he* lied. The good man, my husband, Mr. Edmund Bligh.

Lied from the start, lied about this place, with his 'beautiful', and 'heavenly', and his talk of friendly villagers, and how I would love it. All lies.

It was dark when he brought me here from London to the nearest station, then a trap (yes, a trap!) to the front door. Midnight. So that, for a few hours, I didn't know. True, it was November, the back-end of the year. London had its peasoupers, perhaps it was the same here. But when I looked through the windows the next morning, it was a different light, I knew straight away. I could see nothing, yet somehow I just knew what the mist hid. The grey sea, thrashing up the rocks, trying to get to the mountains behind. The rusting ore of the cliff, the veins of the surface, pooling at the bottom. No golden sand, after all. No blue waves, flecked with white, no gently rising heights, dotted with cotton wool sheep. Nothing beautiful, nothing bright and full of life. No picture-postcard, at all! Back then I didn't understand about the ore, didn't have the words. I do now, for all the good it does me.

'Did you plan it?' she said, sitting beside him, as he lay,

mouthing like the netted goby he fished from the rock pool. 'The weather, when we came here?' Her fingers kneaded the pillow in her hands. 'Another pillow, to make you more comfortable,' she told him. 'It will help your breathing. One more, I think.'

And yes, just as I thought, it was the same day after day.

'It will get better. November is always the worst month,' he told me later. 'Soon, the sunny winter days will come. Cold, yes, but bright.'

'Colder than this?' I asked. 'Cold' was part of the murk. A sodden chill, that draped itself over the house, then seeped in, like the words later, through the rattling window frames, the gaping chimneys, the stone of the walls. Inside, it would cloak my skin, then work its way through my pores to my very core, until I felt I would never be warm again.

'We must have more fires,' I said, through chattering teeth. 'Throughout the house, to build up the heat.'

He looked at me, with those dog-eyes, that oh-so-slightly raised corner of his lip. Already I had come to know that look so well.

'Mother,' he whispered.

Ah, yes, mother. Another of his lies. Well, not so much a lie, perhaps, as a kind of secret – this 'mother' who had scarcely been mentioned whilst he was courting me, seducing me with the attractions of his wonderful home. Mother lived 'there', somewhere, a vague reference. 'There' so that I thought she had her own house, in another part of the village, close, perhaps, but not with us. Not that.

She opened the door to us that first night.

'Still,' I thought, 'he's sent word, and she's just here to warm the house, to get it ready for us.'

But no. She lived there, had always lived there. It had been the house of her husband, until he died and the widow would remain. The reverend mother must remain. It was, after all, hers.

She stood there, all darkness too, dressed in black from head to foot, her widow's weeds, though he'd told me his father had been dead for half his life-time. Was she mourning someone else, I wondered? (Her son, perhaps, that he had been lost to another, to me?) But no, it seemed she had dressed this way for all those mourning years. Different shades, maybe – jet, ebony, sable – but black, always black.

'She'll welcome me, at least,' I thought. 'For 'im, for show, if nothing else.' But no, she drank him with her eyes, and wrapped her arms about him, while for me there was nothing but one swift up-and-down blink from head to toe, getting the measure of me. And that was that. She ushered him through another door, her on one side, a maid on the other, despite his walking well enough in some fashion when he was with me.

'The study has been prepared,' she told him, then shut the heavy door in my face, leaving me to stand there alone, to look about and consider this place I must now call home.

Except I could hardly bleedin' see it. It was lit less than the basements during the Zeppelin raids. There was a feeble oil-lamp, set within an alcove, its flickering sending shadows around the room like they were dancing. The floor was made of toe-numbing slate slabs, damp, that seemed to glue my thin soles to them. The walls were wooden – mahogany, he told me – panels, stretching to the upper ceiling above the stair-well, with prints of Old Testament scenes, all hell-fire and brimstone. 'Is that where I am?' I wondered, 'In Hell, sent here for my sins?' Maybe I'd simply missed the moment of my dying. But then I thought 'No, it's a life-sentence, not death.' In a frozen, sunless, airless prison.

I was still standing there when the maid re-appeared, to show me to my room. She led me up the stairs, along a winding corridor, to a door at the back of the house. A room for one, surely no more than a servant's quarters, with no fireplace, no furniture beyond a narrow bed, a wash-stand and bedside table; a cell within the prison. It is the room I keep to now, seeing it for something else, for sealed rooms can keep out, as well as in. Or used to.

I didn't sleep that night, nor in many of the nights after, as I lay there, listening to the silence.

'Where are the sounds?' Another of my questions for 'later'. He laughed. 'Listen!' he said. I strained my ears. But no, I could hear nothing. No rattle of passing buses and cars, no distant hum of factories, no rush of footsteps, no chattering and giggling snatched outside, no music drifting from the theatres and halls. No sounds of a living place, with living people in it.

'The sea,' he said. True, there was that endless back-and-fore whoosh, with the suck of pebbles following. Or, in rough weather, the crashing on the front.

'The wind,' he said. Yes, there was that, too. Whining, roaring, fussing, nagging at me constantly, like a grouchy mother.

'The birds. Their song…' Yes, I heard the hacking of the crows, broken now and then by some annoying trilling and chirruping, or by the cry of a gull, blown in. Caw, tweet, keeow.

'Rooks,' he said. 'They are rooks, not crows. They have nested in the pine trees for generations, far longer than us. They talk to each other, like all the birds. Such a conversation – they hold a parliament, even! So many of them!'

'Look,' she told him, 'Can you see? I have had the trees cut

down. There will be no more rooks now. There will be no more noise now. But there will be more light, and wood for the fire. Wood for burning.' There was so much to burn. There would be more, soon. So she was glad the rooks were gone, they had seen too much.

Noise, it was – just noise. I missed hearing the city in the beginning, so alien it all was to me. Just noise that didn't belong to the real world, my world, the world of people, and busy-ness, and excitement, and go-getting. So that I dismissed it, and lay in that unreal silence, waiting.

There is a sound. One Grace used to know, but lost during the years of silence. The heavy give of the brass letter-box, the brief flight, the gentlest of landings. Post. But there was no-one to write to her. There had been no-one to write to her before, after they had all given up, stopping their efforts and entreaties to help her and rouse her from her pain.

–All the business of the house has been completed, there should be no further correspondence.

– Why dither? Just go and look.

A cream envelope lies face down on the mat.

'Let it lie,' John tells her as she bends to pick it up. 'It isn't for you.'

'How do you know?'

– How does he know? Better to see. It can't be left there, anyway. Pick it up, turn it over.

But John is right, it isn't for her.

Mrs Esther Bligh.

The sinuous script in deepest black gives the name of someone else entirely. *Mrs Esther Bligh.* There is something familiar about it, a vague recollection just beyond her grasp. The address is the correct one, so the postman has not pushed the letter into the wrong box.

– Perhaps it is someone who lived here before.

'But no-one has lived here for more than twenty years. It's nothing to do with you, Grace. Nothing!'

She turns the envelope this way and that in the dim light of the hall window. It has a weight to it. The paper is of good quality. She traces the letters of the script.

– Feel the indentation of the nib, follow the flow of the

ink, as it draws the letters up and around and back down, in perfect symmetry.

– Such beautiful handwriting. Calligraphy, almost, as they used to teach us in school, before the first war. I haven't seen it since. It is as if the writing and the paper belong to a different age.

– Notice the post-mark. 1924. A letter from all that time ago, reaching here, now! Too intriguing to ignore.

–How could that happen? Where has it been all this time?

– Open it.

Her hand strays toward the flap, her nail flirts with the edge.

'Leave it,' John speaks again. 'Forget about it. Just one of those errors in the postal system. Too long ago to need to put right.'

– Yet there may be a return address. Find the sender, notify them of what has happened. Or go to the post-office, and tell Mrs Evans about it, asking if she knows an Esther Bligh. A reason for a longer conversation than the usual one about the weather. A chance to discuss the history of the place, perhaps.

– Mrs Evans is eighty, at least, has lived here all her life. She will know, if there is anything to be known. She has been quite friendly, on the days I've ventured as far as the shop, though a little more than I would like.

– Natural enough in a small place. Do it… and wouldn't it be better to have as much information about the sender before any enquiries?

Her nail pushes deeper under the flap.

'No!' His voice is raised now, hurting her head. 'I told you to leave it!'

She had promised to love, honour and obey him. It was

what she had always intended to do, throughout their blissful married life together. She would be the perfect wife, seeing to his every need, granting his every wish.

– But your marriage was a two-day honeymoon, and a week-long goodbye, before he was gone.

– Yes, he left you.

– All this time…

– Open it. Open it now!

And she does.

… thief… Spitting in her face.

……………whore. Gouging at her nerves.

…suffocated… pillow…

MURDERER! Clutching at her throat, stealing her breath, like the discarded widow's collar.

'Burn it,' John yells. 'Straight away!'

– NO!

She lays the poisonous words, pushed back into their smooth, heavy wrapper, down on the hall table.

How I long for that silence now. How I'd like to hear nothing but the sounds of nature, the wind, the sea, the birds – all those things I hated before. Instead, the words come at me, even in my tiny room, even though I have laid rugs over the splitting floor, rolled a blanket beneath the door, pushed bits of card into the ill-fitting frames. I leave the heavy shutters tightly fastened day and night, but still they come. Shouting at me, slapping at me, tearing at my ears, no matter how I clutch them with my clenched hands, clenched till my finger-nails cut my palms: but still I hear. Sometimes they are insects on my body, like the fleas in the old places, itching at my skin. They burrow into my flesh, so that I pull at it, ferreting deep, so that red lines score across me, and I bleed, but do not want to bleed, for they can enter now through my veins, and my heart is open to them. Inside me, outside me, everydamnwhere.

Liar… not such a bad word.
Slut. The streets of London are full of them.
Bitch… What woman isn't one?
Whore… What man doesn't buy one?
And…

Harlot. Jezebel. Fornicator. New words for me then, yet meaning much the same. New words – or old… old, old, coming from the Bible, the big, black book that was chained to a heavy, dark pedestal on the first landing, in full view of the hall. Coming from his mother, reading from it morning, noon, and night, ringing out each word like a death-knell, impossible to ignore. She stood there, in her jet crêpe, her widow's cap, her claws hooked over the edge of the book, her voice barking its way through any door or wall I hid behind. I knew she was talking to me, only me. Well, what other woman was there, apart from the toothless, gormless maid? No, I was the harlot, the sinner, the fallen woman. Delilah – one of her favourites. Lot's wife, another... 'Daughter of Sodom!' 'Spawn of the Devil.' On, and on, and on, the stories of their sins. Sin – oh, how she loved that word! 'SSSinnnn!' Oh, how that word followed me more than any of the others. A slippery word, it could slither round doors or through key-holes. Not a hard word, like so many of them, not a word to hit you in the gut like a cheap Saturday night punch – a word, instead, to be slipped into your mouth, where it would choke you.

'She knows,' I thought. 'She knows what I've done against the walls in the alleyways, on rusty springs in the cheap hotel rooms, what I have been doing for years, since I first learnt how it could make fools of men.'

'Do you know what I have done?' she said to him. 'The things men have done to me, and begged me to do with them? Your beloved comrades, your noble 'men', worse than any? Shall I tell you?' She bent closer to him.

Yet, how could she know? How could she know such things happened, when she had lived in this back-of-beyond all her life, been married once, and dried up since – just the one child, somewhere in between, surely by some fluke? And how could she know what I, Esther, had done? She'd not been there!

No, what she knew came from that Book, with its fancy words and names. A Book by men, for men, ruled by The One Man, who blames women for sin. Harlot. Jezebel. Abomination.

Still, she was right, wasn't she, about what had happened

with her beloved son – how he had been caught by the temptress? She read me the moment I walked through the door, as clearly as she read from that Book. Or so it seemed, as she rained curses down on me, damning me, scourging me with nothing but holy words. For that was her greatest pleasure – to follow the tales of the lost women, with whatever fate was brought down upon them from On High. Here was Lot's wife, turned into a pillar of salt. There was another, torn apart by dogs. Elsewhere, so many 'smitten' (how she and the Book liked that word!) by all manner of things – consumption, the sword, madness, blindness – on and on and on.

'Mother's such a kind woman. You will love her. She will love you.'

Bitch. A word for her, not me. Bitch, witch, viper.

Liar. A word for him.

There were days when the bible followed me around the house, I was sure. I told him once, when I thought he couldn't hear. He laughed.

'It smells. Can't smell it? It stinks of age and dried-up cow hide, and dirty clothes. But when it rains, it is worse. And it is always blee… always raining…'

It was true. Smarting inside my nose whenever I passed it – as I had to, whenever I walked up or downstairs. Clinging like a London fog, so that I couldn't escape it, so that I took it with me wherever I went.

'It ain't healthy.'

He laughed again, stroked my hair, and told me it was the family bible, going back generations, that if I were to look inside the cover, I would see the names of his forefathers stretching back years. And my name should be added to it, if mother had not done it already, linked to his for all eternity by a small 'm' and the date of our marriage. And more, if we were blessed, if he should get better, as he was sure he was going to because he had prayed so hard for it, well, perhaps below our names, there would be another. 'It is more than a bible,' he said. 'It is the history of our family.'

Later, when she had gone, I burnt it.

'I tore it, page by page,' she said, watching for his eyes to drown in tears, 'and dropped each one into the stove.' Flare, crackle, melt. There were too many. Besides, perhaps there was more satisfaction in seeing a wodge of Kings, Deuteronomy, Leviticus go up in flames. 'In Hell,' she thought, 'in Hell before me.' She laughed at that. She laughed in front of him. Still, he did not cry. Still there was only pity.

So many words dissolving in flame and smoke. All those names she had slung at me. Jezebel, harlot, whore. All gone. I didn't know then that they would be said again, that I would see them written on fine paper, again and again and again. I didn't understand the way of words – how they could live, even if they were not being said or read; how they could hurt. All I knew then was the pleasure I felt at destroying her precious bible. A proper revenge for the torment she'd inflicted on me.

But all that was later. There were still months of that putrid Book to be endured before then. Months of her sneers and her sniping and smiting. Her stinking presence that I was desperate to escape. But how?

'Where are the shops?' I asked her one day, after I had been shut in that house for what seemed like months, though maybe was no more than two weeks – confined in that dreary prison, with its suffocating air, its bloodless occupants. Outside was no better, no lighter, with the shortest of days, the brunt of the freezing temperatures, and the constant downpours. Still, I thought by then that I must go out, I could stand it no longer. And this day, the rain was not quite a biblical deluge, the wind not fully a tempest sent by the merciful Lord. I would go out, and walk along the 'front' as they called it, and find the centre of this village or town or hellhole, whatever it was, and look around its shops, and sit in a tearoom, watch a film in the Hippodrome, perhaps, and chat to its inhabitants (who were so friendly, I had been told), and it would be a change. And perhaps I could breathe again.

Her lips stretched into an even thinner line – straight, neither up nor down, like a razor cut. She raised one arm, the hand downwards, with the index finger tipped upwards ever so slightly, in some imitation of a pointing action. Left, I took it to mean. What else could it be, in truth, with the cliff wall rising on the right of the house, blocking out all light and air on that side, closing off any means of escape?

I put on my hat of moiré and velvet, trimmed with red roses, my fur coat, decked with my red flouncing scarf, my shiny high-heels – all brand new, that he'd paid for just before we left, never asking what had happened to the money he had given me for my *trousseau*, as he called it, only a few weeks before. A chance to wear them, I thought. A chance for the village people to see what I was: Mrs Edmund Bligh, from the Big House.

Mrs Edmund Bligh, clipping down the road, pulling her coat tighter around her, desperate to keep out the cold, the sluicing rain, desperate to breathe, to take at least one deep breath, to fill her lungs, to clean them of the fug of that airless house, but unable to, on account of that bloody wind. Jesus, that wind whipped against my cheeks, stinging, wet but different from the rivers drowning me. I ran my tongue across my lips, and tasted salt. The seawater was scudding above the wall, smashing against me. The sea, that was there, I knew, to my right, yet I could not see it, with my eyes half-closed by the spray, the mist, the gale.

On I went, no jaunty saunter, or tight-heeled clip, now – no more than a sot's stagger, a buffeting like I got as a kid when Selfridges started up, until I reached what must be the Square, the centre. Nothing but a single shop-front in the lower-floor of a house, with a sign saying 'Post-office and general stores' beneath some nonsense words. And even on this most foul of days, the gossiping shrews were gathered outside it, hat-brims overlapping, gloved hands cupping, clogs tapping – yes, I swear there were some dressed in clogs and flannel, Jesus! And their eyes lifted and stuck themselves to me as I blew towards them, then narrowed to dagger points.

I smiled. I swear – again – that first time I smiled, smiled and nodded. I thought 'I'll try.' What I was trying, I didn't know, but nonetheless, I acknowledged their presence, as I edged past them to the door of the shop.

And they spat at me. That was how it seemed. Their grating, tchhing words hurt my ears, they were spat out between twisting tongues, and sicking-up throats. And there it was again, when I got myself inside, hacked at me now by the post-mistress, real Lady Muck she was, from behind her counter, her lips and double-chins wobbling away. 'Are they all mad?' I wondered. Was this some kind of speaking in tongues, the kind of thing I heard about from the Black Book? And then I understood – or didn't understand, would never understand what was scrabbling at my ears: Welsh. We were in Wales, of course, so this must be Welsh, like the words above the door. Something else he hadn't told me – that his 'friendly villagers' spoke in a foreign tongue.

'English,' I said. 'Mrs Edmund Bligh,' I added.

The woman began again. And still I could not understand her, even though I knew she now spoke in English. There were words that I could latch on to, but her voice went up and down, up and down, in an accent so thick that I could make out no more than one in five. And yet I knew the gist, I knew what she was doing. She was asking me the hows, whens and wheres about myself, and about Edmund, wanting, no doubt, to understand, more than anything, the 'why?', so that she could be superior and repeat it all to her little gang outside. I had known her type before. The buzzing queen bee the hive centred on. I had been stung by such before. I turned and fled.

So this was my choice: to spend my days buried in that prison, guarded by the Mother Superior; or put myself at the mercy of the elements, and of the goggle-eyed, hissing inhabitants, torn between their desire to know every last morsel about me, and their determination to ignore my presence on their sacred earth.

There were one or two days – a half a dozen at most – when daylight worried its way through the heavy drapes. More than light – sun. A fuzzy sun, true, its strength dimmed by the hulking shoulders of the mountains and the crooked arm of the cliff, but, still...

I went out. I went out, not in my fancy coat and my high heels, but in clothes of his I found hanging in the hall. 'Let them think what they like,' I told myself. 'They will think it, anyway. At least I will be warm.'

I went out, and did not turn towards the Square, but walked straight ahead, then down some rugged steps, and down, onto treacherous pebbles that were determined, I was sure, to make me fall or twist my ankle. And then there was dun grit – or sand, as they called it – and then there was sea. A quiet sea for once, a line of lapping foam, rolling gently towards me, asking something of me.

I had been on a beach only once before in my life. 'A treat,' my father said. A treat to have every cranny of my body grubbed and rubbed full of coarse grains, scraping my childish flesh, while he… I had thought I would never be in such a place again. And yet here I was, feet squelching in ooze like the banks of the Thames, lips splitting with salt, eyes watering in the sea-breeze. I sat down, my hand kneading the seeping shingle beside me. I hated it then, I hated it now. And I hated the sea most of all, that I could not enter it, for, of course, I could not swim! That one time before, when I had seen the blue water, I had run away from it, except it had followed me, and caught me, and licked me like an icy tongue, so that I screamed while my father stood and laughed. Then he picked me up and threw me in, and came after…

'If I could swim, I could walk into the water and swim straight ahead to…' Where? Where was I? I hardly knew, beyond 'Wales'.

'See,' he said, as they sat in the railway carriage, moving deeper and deeper into darkness. He put the atlas on her lap, and led her finger around a sea-skirted outline. She watched her reflection smile and nod in the black window, as she listened to the tcktcktck of the train, keeping his words from her. 'Beautiful' and 'wonderful' over and over, but nothing else reached her. 'Do you remember?' she asked him, later. 'Is that really as you see it? This forgotten backwater, this shit-hole? Did you really think I would love it? But then, you thought I loved you.'

And where was that? Even if I had listened to his lectures, would I know what he meant? North, south, east, west – what were they to me? I had lived somewhere to the north of the city, as a child, and now I was west of it, I knew that much. But he had spoken of *peninsulas* and curving coastlines and mountains and valleys. Ireland – there had been mention of Ireland. Was that in front of me? Was that where I could swim to if I just went on and on and on? But what would be the good of that? A bog-sodden wilderness, with nothing but potatoes to eat and not enough of them, and trouble going on in it like a permanent Friday night down the Old Kent Road, a place where even more rain was said to fall.

To the right of me was the cliff, and round from it were the mountains, stretching up and beyond. There was nothing that way. And the other way? Another headland, but somewhere around it was where we had come from. There was a town, though how many miles away I didn't know. And there was a railway, connecting it to another town, and another and another, until surely, finally, it would reach some point of bleedin' civilisation. That was the way I must go. If I could swim. Except I could not swim.

It was all nonsense, of course. And as I sat there, the sun gave up its pathetic fight, with the clouds gathering all around it above the sea, spreading themselves around the cliff top, before they let loose their spit and tears on me again. And the sea was doing that thing it did of coming closer and closer. And it had changed from the lapping to the churning white froth, so that I had to struggle up from the mudsand, and falter my way back up to the road, and in to the house, soaked through my – his – clothes in no more than a few moments.

And his mother opened the door to me, as if she had been watching me, and waiting, wearing that smirk on her face to show she was glad I was dripping and trembling, and that I had nowhere to go, except my poor little room. As if she had already beaten me – this cheap hussy she thought she had understood in that one look on my arrival. This Jezebel who with the help of her Lord she would defeat easily enough. But, no, she did not know me. And neither did she know the true foolishness of a weak man.

There had been another word, snatching at me now and then, distantly caught, then dismissed as the creak of the boards, the sigh of the wind. 'Esther, Esther.' My name. And then, one day, passing through the hall as the doctor was leaving, when the door to the study could not be shut so swiftly, I heard it more clearly. Edmund was calling me. I looked at the doctor and smiled at him. I looked at his mother, and smiled at her. And pushed past both of them to go in.

He lay there on a couch made up as a bed, in a room lined with books and cases and shelves of strange and not so strange objects. Stuffed birds and animals; rocks; bones. There was a large desk in front of the window, and a small table at his side, with a book and some paper on it. His work-room, his study. He wanted to know why I hadn't visited him, and what had I been doing? I told him that I had been advised against it, that I had been told it was better not to excite him. I let him take what meaning he liked from that.

'Well, you're here now. Stay.' So I did.

I went every day then. He thought it devotion, while she knew it for cunning. Well, there was some of that, of course, but there was something else that neither of them considered – it was warm in there. The fire was kept burning in that grate, while the rest of the house was eaten away by creeping mildew and rot. I sat there on a chair placed by his head, and soaked up the warmth, as if I were trying to regain all the heat that had leeched out of me since I had moved to that place. There was more light, too. He needed it, he said, for his reading and his work, the little he could manage. His bed had been pulled around to face the window, overlooking the side of the garden away from the cliff, and the tallest of the trees. It was almost pleasant in there. Better, easily, than anywhere else in the house. So, better to sit there beside him and have to hold his hand now and again, and stroke his hair, and listen to his prattling on and on about things I knew nothing about, nor wanted to know anything – those books, creatures, stones and skulls. And on and on about the future, 'our' future, what we would be doing soon, as he was feeling so much better, it wouldn't be long now. Those words again, those lies again. 'Home,' 'heaven', 'blessed'. I nodded, I smiled. 'Paradise.'

Purgatory.
Hell.
Damnation.

That night, Grace dreams of Esther Bligh. Except she doesn't know who Esther Bligh is.

A woman without a face, without clear form, who wanders through the shadows of a house – *this* house. Sometimes, she carries a child in her arms; sometimes, there is a man, too, who follows her around, calling 'Esther, Esther!' But Esther moves faster, faster, never allowing him to catch up with her, until she disappears.

Sometimes, the figure in her nightmare is no more than a shroud.

Then the words came, the letters breaking apart, some big, some small, tripping down the passageways of the house, behind the fleeing figure.

L i a R. Thieffff. HArlot. W h O R e. WHORE! WHORE! WHORE!

loud, so loud, so that Grace is woken: woken by the shout, and by a heat rising through her, a heat that she has not felt since coming to this perishing house. A heat she has not felt for years and years, and knew only a handful of times in her life, then buried along with her lost husband and her living self. Shame, shame!

It is still the middle of the night. She fights to return to a sleep that wasn't there, to be woken again at dawn, her mouth gaping for air as she tussles to push the pillow away from her face.

'No, not that pillow. I burnt that pillow. Remember?'

Of course, it isn't *that* pillow; something that old would smell musty, and be blotched by mildew in the eternal damp of the house. Yes, the big old cupboards contain piles of linen, belonging to another age, just as the house itself belongs to another age, keeping its relics safe. But this isn't one of them. Instead, it must have been bought for the short time when the house was rented for a holiday season – she knows that from somewhere, she thinks.

– But this bed, this room? Perhaps?

– It made sense to come in here, didn't it?

– Later, perhaps, it will be needed for the guests. But for now, why should I not be in here? The best room – the best view, at the front facing the sea.

– Catching the weather.

– Well, yes, but still, the lightest—

– Though still dingy, on account of the heavy furniture, the over-wrought patterned wallpaper—

– True, but I can change that. I will change it. In time. For now—

For now, she is in the four-poster bed in the main bedroom, the great bed for the husband and wife of the house.

– Is that the real reason you chose it?

As if she and John had come back here, as planned? John… John whose voice told her not to read the letter.

– But you did. Why shouldn't you, if you want?

– 'Burn it, Grace. Burn it!' he said.

– But you didn't.

– Come on. Do it now. It is foolishness, these thoughts, nightmares. What was the letter, after all? A wicked prank, perhaps, the writer being the sinner, the liar, bent on the torment of a fragile mind.

– And even if true, those involved are long dead, surely. To ask the post-mistress is foolishness. Better to let sleeping dogs lie. Better to forget all about it.

– Get up, go downstairs, pick up the letter from where it lies. And the envelope – burn that, too.

Of course, it is one of the days when the stove is out, not a single sickly ember struggling to stay alive inside. She will have to start afresh.

– And today, there are no sticks in the basket; you will have to go outside to fetch some. And outside is wet, as usual.

– Just put the letter in and light it with a match. The fire can come later.

She starts to crumple the paper in her hand.

– And yet… a shame to burn such beautiful writing; just as it is a shame that such beautiful writing was used to shape such venomous words. Perhaps you missed something. Last night, you gave it no more than a glance.

Yes, it was true; she had barely taken in anything but the words that leapt from the page and hit her in the face, and wrenched her inside.

– Read it more carefully. Perhaps it will look different then.

She smooths out the paper, sits down by the dead fire and reads.

'Dear Esther Bligh,' that is how it begins – no address, no date. 'Esther Bligh', written as on the envelope in that enticing sinuous script, the letters curving and looping and curling, as if the writer was indulging their art. E. B.

– Something familiar about those initials, that name. Something… something in this house, maybe. Go and look.

– NO, not now. Keep reading now. Read what they have to say.

– But who is 'they'?

– A woman, surely, from the hand, the style… the tone. But there is no signature, the only name on the letter is 'Esther'.

– You saw this last night, when the words lashed out at you, and you turned the single page. An anonymous letter, a poison pen letter.

She knew of such things, just as she knew such words existed in lives other than hers. Lives far away from the tree-lined avenue where she lived, with its houses for retired solicitors and the widows of bank-managers, such as Mother. Houses with high, neatly-trimmed hedges to keep them safe and apart. The road ended at the entrance of a large park, separating it from the other side of town, the 'wrong' side – somewhere she was told she must never go.

– Whore, bitch, harlot. Harsh words, scrabbling, scratching at your ears, just as they scored into the cream paper, leaving deep ruts of ink doused in black venom. BITCH.

– Don't read it, don't see what comes next, what you saw last night, but tried to deny.

– Liar, thief, slut. Not that. Not those words. They are nothing – no reason to 'burn in Hell', to 'suffer every earthly punishment' on account of those.

– Read it, read what Esther has done.

– A pillow, a pillow pressed to his face, as he lay in the marriage-bed.

– There is something else, see, see it now.

– A child, a dead child, no more than a baby.

– Murderer. Worse than all the other words put together. The worst word of all.

Words come with pictures. Not just lines and curves, forming letters, making words. The shadow of a girl, standing on a corner, red lips puckering towards her prey.

A hand, a sleight of hand, slipped into a pocket.

Arms holding a baby, and then the baby is dead.

A pillow, the woman holding it, down, down.

A match. She must get a match. She must do as John told her, and burn the letter.

– I shouldn't have read it. I should have listened to him. I wish I had never seen it, and read the words.

– But you have, haven't you?

– There are the matches, and the stove is right there. Open it, put the paper in, set it alight, burn it. That's all there is to do.

– But—

– There!

The first doesn't light, nor the second.

– The damp, like everything here.

Or a draught, from somewhere she cannot see.

But the third flares, long enough to hold its yellow flame against the paper. A brown-lipped bite eats away at the pale edge, then fades, along with the stain.

Another match, another flame – how many times? – the rust spreading, brown to black to nothingness. And then, finally, it catches properly, yellow turning to orange, to red, as it leaps and dances through the page.

Warmth, a gasp of heat. She cannot lose what is so rare in this place, no matter where it comes from, so sits, with the stove door wide, reaching her hands to its source.

The paper curls in on itself, then loses itself in a rush of flame. It is one page, and now that it has caught, it will be gone in a moment. And yet…

A word. The worst of the words, again. She sees it, rising with the smoke, clinging to the grey wafts, as if desperate to hang on, as it meanders towards the black mouth of the flue.

– It can't be. There's nothing, your imagination, again. Forget about it all. It's gone, all gone.

And now, yes, the flame and the smoke have given up,

and all that is left is a mound of dove-grey flakes, so light that if she blows on them, she knows they will dissolve to nothingness. All gone, but for one word, still plain on its untarnished background. Murderer.

Grace shrinks away from it, deeper into the sagging armchair. An unlikely chair for this cheerless, functional kitchen, full of tarnished cast-iron and stark wooden furniture.

A step. A push. A flutter. A landing. The postman is there again. This early, while she is still sitting by the range, pushing the poker into the ash, mashing that last shred of poison to dust. Gone, all gone now; no more of this. Just a silly episode, a nonsense. Why is she bothered about it? She won't be bothered about it! It is finished.

She goes to the hall, to see what the post has brought today. An old envelope, addressed to Mrs Esther Bligh, the same as before, lying on the fraying rush mat, held together by the grime of the years.

Mrs Esther Bligh, Mrs Esther Bligh, Mrs Esther Bligh. They come every day now, all the same. The same paper, the same writing, the same content – or much the same; a change in the detail here, a different choice of words there. Sometimes, a paragraph will digress into a specific story of Esther in this place. 'Do you remember that day…?' 'I have never forgotten the time when…'

– So the writer must be from here, and came across Esther in her daily life.

She reads each letter as it comes, and dreams about Esther every night.

'Don't,' John tells her again. 'Burn them!' he yells.

But somehow she can't help it. Each day she sees the letter there, and lifts it from the floor, her fingers toying at the sealed edge before his words arrive. Besides…

– What if it is different this time? A new kind of letter, entirely, apologising for the others, saying there has been the most terrible mistake.

– It has all been a mistake…

– Perhaps.

– Or perhaps this one will be signed, so that you know where it comes from. Better to open it, just in case.

– Or…

And soon John is quiet, along with all the other voices, except for the one – the sweet voice that told her to open the first letter, the voice that is now her constant companion. She thinks.

– Read it. Read them all. Read the words. Whore, bitch, slut. Harlot, Jezebel, witch. Murderer…

The word is purring almost, lingered over, the 'mur' murmured and stretched out, lovingly.

– Not such a bad word, after all.

On the third day, Grace catches the postman, waiting for him in the front-room window, then dashing out as he reaches the door. He stumbles backwards, tangling his bag in the hydrangea, before righting himself, and staring at her, scratching his head. 'Beth ti…? Did you…?' No more than a lad, saved from the war by his youth.

'I am not Mrs. Esther Bligh, I am Grace Marlowe,' she tells him. 'There is some mistake. Can you not bring them any more? Please.'

He tells her it is his job; he has to deliver to the specified address.

'Just put them in the bin,' he says. 'Or burn them. Free paper for you!'

'I…' What can she tell him? That she has read them, and they said the most terrible things? Or that she could not burn them, after that first one, no matter how she tries. How it is as if something stays her hand, as she reaches the letter to the stove? About the voices, and this voice that stays with her, saying the words? About her nightmares, and the way the words…

'I…'

He is looking at her strangely already, backing away down the path. She lets him go, and shuts the door.

Ah.

A… hush?

Not silence – no, there is never that. But every now and then, it comes – a respite, a kind of pause, when the words are held at bay, still there, but distant. So that I can snatch a few scant hours of sleep, eat a bite (perhaps). Breathe. Yes, it happens, but never lasts long. Not any more. And the intervals get fewer and further between. But… still…

There was a lull of sorts, then. A spell of calm, you might say. I would sneak past the talking tome (one of his words, that!), hands together, head bowed, ears shut. 'Perhaps she will think I am *penitent*,' I thought. Not in a month of Sundays… And I would slip into the study, and sit there with him, acting the doting wife.

Sometimes, I would take my sewing with me. A skill with the needle was the only thing my mother gave me, and it had served me well enough until I realised there was an easier and more profitable trick. By some miracle, I had discovered a bundle of harlequin quilts in the back of the linen-cupboard, never used, never wanted by the matron of the house, who preferred to revel in funereal misery; they made me think of the halls, and the comics and play-actors, and the singers. So I worked to re-fashion them into splendid new outfits I told him would be suitable for my position as Mrs Edmund Bligh, in this oh-so-sociable place we lived in, whilst seeing in my mind Esther Thorpe sashaying down the Mall, as I clung to the belief I would get back there sometime. Somehow…

And then, one morning, from nowhere, he announced

that he would teach me to read! Shame that he should have done so! A *cruel irony* in it! For if he had not, if I had remained in my state of blissful ignorance, the letters that assault me would be no more than inky lines and curves on pieces of paper, a hotch-potch of squiggles like tiny jellied eels in front of my eyes. For that was 'writing' before he took me in hand.

He knew, of course – had known almost from the day we had met, and had pitied me for it, and – another *irony* – it had improved me, rather than diminished me, in his eyes; improved me because he felt he could improve me.

'Poor bird, poor, pretty bird,' he had said to her. 'Do you remember how you thought I should be pitied? Do you still think it now, knowing what I have done? What I am going to do?' She raised the pillow towards him.

At least he never asked me why, imagining some suffering on my part – illness, or forced employment at too young an age, rather than my own choice to bunk off school, in search of more pleasurable endeavour.

And so it began. 'You are so clever, so quick, it won't take long.' There were children's books still on those shelves, his Royal Readers from childhood that his mother kept, in the same way as she kept everything. Clever, maybe, quick, maybe, but oh, so impatient, so bored, as he would take my finger in his hand, and lead it around those shapes, and sound each word out, mouthing them as if to an idiot, gazing at me with those devoted eyes, then praising my each and every success as if he were throwing a biscuit to a dog.

'Warmth,' I told myself. 'Remember the warmth, that it is so much warmer in here than any other room in the house, except, maybe, the kitchen, where the company is the imbecile house-maid.'

'His mother,' I thought. 'She won't like it that he and I

are brought closer by this. Or that I am becoming *educated*, and will soon be a more suited companion for him. Not an ignorant little street tramp now!'

And it came to me, too, that perhaps it was not such a bad thing. I had managed so far without these skills (for the reading was to go hand in hand with writing, of which I had learnt nothing beyond signing my name), living on my wits and wiles, but there were times I had wished for them, thinking they would give me some advantage. And might that not hold true in the future, that future back in London, because I knew with so much certainty that the future could not be here?

Fool – not him, then, but me.

But not when it came to learning, it seemed. He was right. It was soon done. Once I applied myself, it was quick enough. A B C, in big, bold letters, A for Apple, B for Ball, C for Cat; then the children's books put away, volumes one to six. Abc written closely, longer words, harder words; the Cat On The Tree, The Bird's Song; 'Good, good, good. My clever Esther, my sharp little bird!' Then grammar, too, with Mr Alfred West and his 'Elements of English', with nouns, verbs, adjectives. Soon, the bible appeared on the table between us. Not the same giant volume that his mother read from, but a smaller one, with tiny script and flimsy pages. I could not believe that I was reading from the bible! The Good Book, the fount of all wisdom, *her* own favourite. And yet the verses he chose for me to recite were nothing like the burning coals she offered from her pulpit on the landing. Where were the wicked women, the hell-fire and eternal damnation? Instead, there was goodness and love and good deeds, Jesus saves, and all his little lambs.

'The New Testament,' he said. 'The words are more familiar, easier, perhaps, to start with.'

'To start with...' As if I would be going on and on and on. And so it was! This book, that book, pointed at with his stick for me to fetch down, and peer into to.

'Dip into,' he liked to say. 'Today, we shall dip into the Macaulay, Esther.' Or 'why not try a little of the Shakespeare this afternoon? I am sure you will enjoy it. And later, the Wordsworth, or the Tennyson.'

For, apparently, from reading and writing came knowledge. This was the next thing – that I must *know*, learn about the things he knew about, so that we could be as one. Or some such shit.

'I am opening the world for you, Esther,' he said, as I bent my head over his Britannica or the Gibbon. Or his Gould's 'Birds of Asia', or his Audubon, or Hooker's 'Flora of the British Isles', or India, or wherever. These were his favourites – books about animals, plants, birds. *Nature.* 'My subject,' he said, 'that I studied in Oxford.'

'Look!' Oh, the first of so many 'looks!' Look at this picture – a bird; look at that picture – a flower; look at that... the inside of something, a diagram close up, that I did not understand, I had no wish to understand. 'Do you see?/See how/Look closely...' No, I didn't see, but I pretended, as I always pretended back then, needing to be sure of him, feigning interest, just as I had feigned interest in him.

'Isn't it wonderful?'

'Yes, it is wonderful!'

Picture after picture, word after word after word, book after book.

'Look!'

There were books, even, that he had written! He was an expert in the study of some tiny plant or other, so had made a book of it, as well as one on general natural observation.

'Strange, how you never saw the truth in me, you, who were so clever in seeing the world around you. Strange, how you didn't see this coming.' The pillow moving closer...

And so it went on: the education of Esther Bligh. Day after day after day...

There were moments when I was left in peace, when he could finally talk no longer, and he would apologise for his weakness, and lay his head upon the pillow ... *Not that pillow, of course not that pillow*...and close his eyes. He would sleep then, if it could be called sleep, just as the peace I had was hardly quiet. Soon, he would start to tremble and shudder, then toss and turn. With sweat on his brow, his fingers would grab at the edge of the coverlet, and the moaning would begin. A baby's grizzling to start, then, perhaps, the names of men he had seen die. 'No, no, no, not Jonny, or Lawrence', or whoever. 'The blood, the mud, the gas, can't breathe, can't breathe.'

Bleedin' hell. I would watch him then, and think how pathetic he was. I would watch him, and think perhaps he would yet snuff it, like those men. This place would be mine, and I would throw the old cow from here, with her bible tumbling after, laughing as she went. Then I would sell the house and take all his money and go back to the city, go wherever I wanted and... Then the moans would turn to a scream and he would wake himself up, and smile, and take my hand, and tell me that for me, *because* of me, he would soon be better.

Before long, his body was stronger, his sleeps were calmer. Sometimes, then, I would move away from my place by his bed, and go and sit close by the hearth. I would reach my hands out towards the fire, twisting them this way and that, twisting one shoulder, then the other, nearer to the heat, trying to feel that warmth on every part of me so that the ice would go from my veins, from my bones, from my soul, if I had one of those. I would watch the flames, the yellows, the orange, the reds – blue and purple, even, frolicking over the coals, up, down, back and fore, like a music-hall closing number. Such colour, such brightness, so different from the gloaming all around me. Perhaps I dozed myself, then, and saw a figure in a dress of rainbow colours, dancing, twirling round and round, pirouetting in the centre of the hall, a blade of light beamed upon her, the men around her like bees to honey… And then I would hear him sigh, and I would rush back to my place.

'Esther, my Esther.'

'I am here, Edmund. I am here. Always.'

Liar.

Bitch.

And a fool.

She is here, somewhere, Grace is sure. Esther Bligh, E.B. *E.B.*

– There are signs, somewhere, I am sure. I have seen… something.

But not here, on the first landing, where she finds herself sitting after the postman's visit, the latest letter open on her lap. A peaceful spot, where a small chair is conveniently placed in a narrow recess. She looks away from the words, looks through the side-window. There is nothing for her to see, with the glass sluiced by rain on the outside and stained from age within. Still, she knows what is there – a narrow slice of sky and wall, bordered by the cliff. It was where she had sat with John, but she still can't remember seeing this place. It hadn't mattered, then.

Her breath steams the glass in front of her, fogging it even more. The letter falls to the ground, as she hugs herself, rubbing her hands up and down her arms. Sometimes, the cold is good to her, stopping her thinking of anything else. And there is something soothing about the rhythmic up/down, up/down, and the feeling of someone holding her tight. She will stay here for a while, for the rest of the day perhaps. Quiet, alone.

But soon her teeth set hard together, and the chafe of her hands makes no difference, as the ice settles in her bones.

– Get up, put a coat on. You must.

So she does, stepping into the bedroom, only yards away. And at once, the silence ends.

– She is here, isn't she?

– Yes! Here, on the back hem of the drab, dust-clogged curtains, E.B. embroidered…

– Such neat stitches, see! The skill… Perfect!

– Yes.

– Look again, go from room to room. Look carefully.

– The linen cupboard on the second landing. Go up and look there, too.

– Table clothes, antimacassars, cushion covers. Such fine work! All initialled in the corners. But no pillow-cases. Not one.

She burnt those, too. The outer slip that touched his face, pressed down onto his skin. The imprint of his pitying eyes was etched upon it, still looking at her, as she watched it burn. And the gloves. She had put gloves on, so that it was not her skin, her flesh, that touched…

E.B. E.B. E.B. Initials stand for a name. Letters, not words.

– Letters come before words, must be added together to make words; sentences, paragraphs, chapters; whole books.

– Books.

– yes, in the room at the front of the house, full of shelves, the books still mouldering in them. See!

She is there now, somehow, come down the stairs and through the door and standing in the middle of the floor.

She takes one of the books down, then another, and another. 'Esther Bligh', written on the inner cover, 'Esther' above a word crossed out. 'Edmund'; Grace can just decipher it.

– 'Edmund Bligh'. Is Edmund the husband, the dead husband, the husband…?

– And look, look inside. Turn the pages, one, two, four. Chapter Three, Chapter Five.

Single pages gone, carefully unpicked, stitch by stitch. Whole chapters torn away, jagged teeth, biting into the words. Exquisite illustrations scribbled over, in childish fashion, or ripped in two. Irreplaceable volumes of great value ruined.

– Shame, shame on you!

Once upon a time, between the silence and the voices, she had begun to read – a pleasure remembered from childhood, first, on Mother's knee, with the gentle voice talking her through the pictures; then, on her own, her favourite pastime. Returned to then, in search of solace. And, yes, it was the closest she came to peace in that troubled time.

– John had a library like this. I would sit in there, and choose any book off the shelves, and lose myself in it, for a while, at least.

Sometimes, tears blurred the words in front of her, and what she read was nothing to her, no more than her eyes moving from left to right, down, over. Then they had reached her, but she had soon forgotten them. Until finally, it was right again: the words made sense, and stayed with her, becoming her friends. So, too, did the characters in the stories. She grew closer to some of them than she had ever been to real people, except Mother, and then John. For many years they had given her comfort, happiness, sympathy, an outside world brought brightly into that closed, dark house.

'Books are our friends,' he said. She told him what she had done to them. 'Look,' she said, going downstairs and returning with his Audubon. She opened it at the gouged humming-bird, the torn finch, the empty passages. 'Look, see, look!'

– Books were my only companions, until the voices came. Such a shame… Who would do such a thing? Sacrilege…

Sacrilege… the Nazis had burnt the books of their

enemies. 'We should have known,' people said later. 'We should have known what was to come. Only the Evil do such a thing.'

– Sacrilege. A word from the letters…

Who had done this thing?

She knows. She knows it is Esther. She sees her, standing, perhaps, just where she stands, smiling as she works to remove a single page, before throwing it on the fire.

– Bitch.

Another of the chosen words. Only, *Grace* has said it, a word she has never uttered before. It tastes strange in her mouth. She runs her tongue around her lips, and the inside of her cheeks, then shakes her head and walks away.

But Esther follows her now. Or she follows Esther.

– You touched these walls, didn't you?

… as she runs her hands along the mahogany panels in the hall.

– Your feet trod these boards

… as she moves around the kitchen…

– Opened this door, climbed these stairs, looked in this mirror.

…and…

– You slept in this bed…

The Esther of her nightmares is clearer now. Sometimes, she sits by the hearth, quietly doing her needlework; sometimes, she is tearing a book apart; sometimes, she is reading a letter, then burning it. And sometimes, the pillow beneath Grace's head begins to thrash and writhe, as Esther hovers above her.

– Just like before.

So the winter was somehow got through. The long, bleak days endured, broken by a few walks to the town, where the women still gawped and gossiped and spoke in tongues – about me, I knew it was always about me, never *to* me. Not once did they smile towards me, or nod, or say 'Good morning.' Yes, the post-mistress uttered strangled pleasantries, spraying her words over me, but only because I was Mrs Edmund Bligh, and a customer. There was no warmth in it, I was certain. Besides, what was she but a fucking shop-owner?

And then it was Spring, he said. I hadn't noticed it. The heavens opened almost every day, ice still feathered the windows, inside and out, except in his room. The days seemed no longer, the light no brighter. But what did I know? In London it got warm or cold or hot, but things didn't grow and turn and bud; and rutting went on all the time. These seasons and weather and such like were another part of his vast knowledge, that must be deferred to. And he was better, he announced. Not well, of course, but better, and fit enough to go out on the milder, dry days.

'Some exercise and the fresh air will be good for both of us, Esther. And I will be able to show you the place.'

Had I missed something, I wondered? Was there another part of town hidden behind, with proper shops, tearooms, pubs, the Hippodrome, frequented by human beings who liked such things and talked in my own tongue?

I should have known by then who this Mr Edmund Bligh was…

'Out' began with the beach… no, not quite the beach…

First, there was the garden. 'How I have longed to show you the garden, Esther!'

It seemed that my education was to continue in practice now, rather than the book-learning. The painted birds became flesh. 'Look!' He would clasp my arm as we tottered around the place, I wedged beneath his shoulder, like some kind of living crutch. 'There! On the trunk of the tallest pine!' And I would look, expecting to see at least one of the rare visitors he had taught me could sometimes drift even this far west. And it would be a sparrow. Or a blue tit. A magpie. And he would list their characteristics, the difference between sexes, their chosen food etc, etc., whilst I had to mm and ahh, and pretend I was interested… in a robin.

Flowers – that was another one. Before, I had seen flowers as something a man might give you. That was how I judged them, roses being the dearest and therefore the most desirable. But there we would be, walking around his 'beds', and suddenly, he would struggle to his knees, almost collapsing me with him in the process. 'Look, look.' And all I could see was some tiny, pale, cowering bud. 'How could you wrap some tissue and a bow around that?' I would think. 'How could you stand it in a vase?', while he murmured 'beautiful, so beautiful!'

All this, in a square of grass, some earth and some trees. So much more, then, when we finally staggered from the gate, and down on the rickety beach. So much more to 'look, look' at, so much to learn. Pebbles, shells – seaweed, even! Yes, sodding seaweed! He thought seaweed was beautiful, as if he did not understand what the word 'weed' meant. 'You can tell the weather with it,' he said, gathering *pustulating* strands to take home. The sea itself. The sand itself, 'millions and millions of coloured treasures; plant and animal together. Another world beneath the microscope lens!' All these things were sources of adoration, subjects of my education, objects of my derision and despair.

A secret – there was something I almost liked about the shells. They were pretty little things, and I have always liked pretty little things, like the baubles on a street market, sparkling for the punters and the mugs. Some were like tiny cones, some so pale, so delicate, transparent, like the porcelain tea-set his mother kept behind glass-doors, locked away from light-fingered daughters-in-law. Pastel pink, and soft grey, pearly white. Others were bigger, shaped strangely. 'Hold it to your ear,' he said, 'and you will hear the sea.' I did it to please him, though the sea was no more than yards away, and I could hear it plainly. 'Yes,' I said. 'Yes!' Oyster shells, moon shells, scallop shells. 'A razor shell, you can see why.' Long, thin, just like the blade of a barber's tool, and just as sharp. I ran my finger along it. 'Don't,' he said. 'Be careful!' A fine line of blood rose on the surface. 'See, see what you've done! Poor Esther.' The tiniest of cuts, so little blood. He took my finger and put it in his mouth, and sucked it. 'There!'

I liked this shell even more than the others. I put it in my pocket, and took it home, and put it on the small table in my room. He was pleased, taking it as a sign that I was interested,

'I will shave you,' she said. 'To save the nurse. And, after all, I am your wife.' She was careful, caressing his neck with the blade. Up, down. She held the blade above the vein. One cut. There would be no faint pink line, as with the shell. Red, deep, so much blood.

liking any sign that I was interested, that I was sharing his 'wonder of nature', his 'awe at the natural world', while helping him on the path to returned strength and health.

'There is no doubt, Esther, that your love heartens me, and the hope of our future keeps me determined to be well!' Oh, so often did he say it – so often that I wanted to puke – reminding me always of the 'future', in which all I had was more of this, months, years, stretching out in front of me. 'Look, Esther!' 'Yes, Edmund!' on and on and bleedin' on.

On and on, on the beach. Then on and on, up the mountain, when he was well enough to struggle further. New territory for him to drool over – rocks and stones and clouds were presented and explained. I could not believe that there was so much to tell about hard chunks of earth, and fluffy cotton-wool in the sky! 'Clouds – they're just clouds,' I thought. 'We had them in London!' What could be so special about clouds? But these, too, it seemed, could be used to tell the weather. Well, yes, black clouds meant rain, even I knew that. But no, there was far more than that. And there were so many different kinds with their strange names – this 'us', that 'us'. 'Latin,' he said, as if it was something that should excite me, as if it was another language I might like to learn! As for the rocks, that had been there for millions of years, well, so much to say… fact after fact after bleedin' fact.

So here, there, and everywhere we went, with everything crammed into a few fine days, because, I swear, that's all there were – a half-dozen at most.

Sometimes, as we staggered around the place, the village children would appear, or not – sometimes I would see no more than eyes, peeping through a bush or from around a boulder, or hear a rustle on the path behind. But sometimes a crowd of them would openly follow us – dirty, scruffy little things like the urchins, bare-footed, even! who pointed and laughed and shouted in their garbled tongue. And Edmund would stop, and smile at them, and say 'bore ray dah,' or whatever it was, and dig in his pockets for pennies. 'Fool,' I would think, 'he should be yelling at them, or throwing stones, to rid us of their cackling faces. Or running after them with a big stick.' Except he could not run.

Well, I would have done it, had I been on my own, if I had not been with Mr. Edmund Bligh, acting the part of his good lady wife.

Sticks and stones, sticks and stones. It was what the children needed. It was something else, belonging to childhood, theirs and mine. A rhyme we knew from the school-yard, from the back alleys where we played. A rhyme taught to us by our mother, to mock the pain of the names we were called, on account of our rags, and our snot noses, and our drunken father. 'Sticks and stones may break my bones, but words will never 'urt me!' So I would shout it at the chanting girls, as I slapped their faces and kicked their shins. And I would yell it at my sister, when she called me a liar or a slag. And then, to prove it, I would twist the skin on her arm, or pinch her hand. 'See,' I would say. 'The red mark? See your flesh all paining? Yet there's nuffin' on me!' But there was something inside that I kept hidden from her, something heavy, low in my stomach, so that I would wonder then if my mother was right.

Still, in time, I got used to the words, just as I got used to the sticks and stones – because, of course, I had those, too. The cane, my father's hand, the slaps, kicks and pinches returned. I got used to them, and had come to believe that words were nothing but puffed air, or wriggling ink, until they were rained down on me, pummelled into me, forced down my mouth, and every other hole, until I am battered and bruised, blacker and bluer than any stick could make me. Words coming at me, from everywhere and everyone.

Anyone and anybody, it could be. Man, woman, child. Yes, children, too. Even they assault me.

Is it the younger siblings of those sneaking buggers who now hide beneath the wall, or creep beneath the lower windows, then leap up to gurn at me? Or trail after me, down the street, when I have no choice but to go out, and catcall after me, nonsense names, until one, older perhaps, will slip in a word borrowed from the letters – slut, bitch – not the worst of the words, but still enough to make me turn around and scuttle back indoors, back to the darkness of the house that I once was so desperate to leave?

There was somewhere else we must go, now that we could go 'out'. Another mind-numbing, benighted, unfriendly place, where I must put up with the stares, and the raised hands, and the threat of eternal punishment, uttered by the big, black Book, by another one robed in black. Yes, the Church, every Sunday as soon as Edmund could walk that far, with Mother on one side, and me on the other. Not the serving maid. She, it seemed, went to the Chapel, where the raggedy children and the biddies from the Square went, too. We would pass the painted front, with its big door brimming, hear the blaring of song, and then be swallowed by the other house of God, where only a few of the straight-laced gathered to listen to the endless drone of the vicar's sermon and prayer. I saw then where Mrs Bligh received her inspiration, as sin and misery rained down on hard chairs and stone floors and starched collars. And I learnt for the first time of the division of the town, with its Welsh/English, Chapel/Church, poor/rich, and of how I was supposed to thank God that I was one of the shivering few, and pray to him to save my wicked soul, to be worthy of my blessings. My blessings... to be Mrs Edmund Bligh, stuck in this place, that house, with this husband, that woman… 'Dear Lord,' I would whisper, head bent towards the altar. 'Dear Lord, grant me my salvation, take me away from here.'

But I did not believe in the Lord. Whatever I had got in life, I got for myself. Esther Thorpe. Now Esther Bligh… it was she who must find the way. And she would. I was sure. Then.

– Go out. Stop this, and get out of the house. Walk to the post-office and speak to the post-mistress.

– But the weather is still awful, and the letters are still coming.

– Stop reading them. Burn them straight away!

– But what if the next one is different? What if the next one is signed? What if—

– Stop looking for Esther about the place. Stop thinking about her!

– But—

But yes, finally, Grace finds herself walking along the front, bent against a wind that works to push her back towards the cliff, back into the house. At least, she thinks it is the wind. What else could it be? But she keeps on, clutching one of the envelopes in her pocket. She has not brought a letter – just an envelope.

– That is enough, isn't it? There is no need to share all the words. Better to keep them to ourselves for now.

– I suppose.

'Boray dah. Shoo my?' More unfamiliar sounds for her to try on her tongue. Just a greeting, though; nothing evil, yet perhaps she shouldn't, perhaps she will offend. She is glad to be the only customer. But Mrs Evans smiles at her, her ruddy cheeks dimpling deep in their folds, and says 'Dah ee-ow-n, deeolth,' or something like that.

'These letters,' she begins, 'I keep on getting them. But they're not for me. And the post-mark. More than twenty years…'

She puts the envelope on the wooden counter, its surface worn from years of leaning elbows, and smooths it out.

'Esther Bligh' uncreases itself for the post-mistress to see. The smile drains from the woman's mouth, Grace is sure, but she shakes her head.

'No… I… before my time.'

'But I thought…'

'No, no.'

'I think, maybe, … was there ever a …' Her lips falter at the word, as if she will accuse the whole town of the sin, not just Esther. But a murder would be remembered, would have become part of a place's history. '… a murder here?'

She has said the wrong thing, she sees at once. She should have kept quiet, she should have kept this word hidden. But it is too late. The face of the woman behind the counter shuts down, just as she shuts the counter-window down, and the hatch, turning away and muttering 'we are closed now,' leaving Grace standing there, so that all she can do is turn away, too, bits and pieces of words still coming out of her mouth, lost to no-one but herself. Again.

Or do the old women gathered outside, as they always seem to be, catch something of what she is saying, catch a phrase with their outstretched ears, locking a sentence in their hearts and minds, filling in the gaps of her broken conversation?

She nods towards them, but the gesture is defeated by the wide brims of their hats and their rain-streaked spectacles.

It's easier to go back, with the breeze behind her – as if the house is where she's meant to be, as if it's the only place for her. And then there in front of her she sees a sign pointing to the right, showing her the way to the church.

Why not? Some peace, perhaps; shelter from the weather, if nothing else. But the building is hewn from the mountain, with the inside a frozen cavern; an angry God and a crucified

Jesus of black bog oak look down on her, so there is nothing to lift her heart. It was not so different from the church she and Mother had attended, going dutifully every week, as all their neighbours seemed to do, dressed in their Sunday best. She supposed she accepted the words of the Testament in those days, but after the death of her mother, taken by illness so suddenly, she was not so sure. Then, after John… how could she believe in such a cruel god and his religion? The coming of the voices had given her some hope, but that was nothing to do with this place. Still, she can pray, can't she, even though she doesn't believe, she can ask for help from… something. 'Please!'

And, almost at once, she is answered. Words are falling down on her from on high, echoing in the vaulted space, from wall to wall. Words cartwheel towards her, from the open bible that lies on the pulpit at the altar front; words that speak of damnation, and the devil's torment, and the flesh's abomination: sin – words that offer no comfort at all. She clasps her hands to her ears, and stumbles away.

– I told you not to go.

– Did you?

Did she? But who is 'she'? This one voice that stays close by, whilst all the others have retreated to the shadows. The sweet voice, only it is not always so sweet any more.

– I told you the people here were mean and unfriendly.

– Did you?

– Someone said.

– Who was that?

– Was that you?

Words inside her mind, outside her mind, words and sounds, muddling and confusing.

– Are you you?

Sugar drips through silk-lined lips, then grates and scrapes.

And yet, somehow, she must still listen.

Listen, as the voice still tells her to read every letter, the letters that still arrive every day.

– Read it! Read them!

– But they are all the same, now.

Round, and round and round.

Bitch. Whore. Whore, bitch, slut. Liar, thief. Murderer, slipped in, or shouted loud. Harlot, Jezebel, she-devil, slut. Whore, bitch, round and round and round. Until…

– What…?

Another letter. Another addressed to Mrs. Esther Bligh.

– But the writing is different, nothing like the elegant calligraphy.

– Child-like, almost, and written in biro, on thin, bluish-white paper. The post-mark still belongs to the local sorting-office…

– But the date. Look at the date.

The date is from two days ago.

– 'Dear Esther Bligh' again. No signature, again.

But between the greeting and the nothingness, there is a slap-dash scrawl, with crossings-out and arrows forcing missed letters between mis-spelt words. But the old words are still there. Bitch, whore, slut. And 'you did this, you did that, we know' is there.

– Someone from the village, someone from 'now', knows what Esther Bligh did, or might have done. And they know about the letters from long ago, and they are copying them in their fashion. Why?

– Why?

– I told you. I told you what they were like, how they eavesdrop and gossip and interfere.

– Did you?

– Yes. And now one of them has written this.

– I suppose…

– Well, who else could it be?

– Not the post-mistress. Not her.

– But she must have repeated what you told her. Or those women outside overheard—

– Yes, a woman, another woman. Someone who sits there hour after hour, with nothing better to do; someone who thinks she is being clever, perhaps?

– And this, now, is directed at *you,* not Esther Bligh, because this woman must know that Esther is dead, that the only person who can open the letter is Grace Marlowe – you. Only you can open it, and read it. Read the cruel words.

– Someone is mocking you. Taunting you. Hurting you. Somebody wants … what?

And now the letters mingle present with past, fluttering or tumbling down to the mat, like so many feeding birds. Different birds, different writing, all these new words sent to her, along with those from long ago. Different, but the same.

Words worm into the house. Watching, she sees them as they slink down the road, and creep through the letter-box, into her mind. One day, she takes a piece of cloth, and stuffs it into the brass slot. The postman will give up, surely, and take the letters away. But the next morning, the rag lies there on the mat, and the words lie there again. The letter-box is like a mouth, ever open, spewing hate. And once inside, there is no escape.

She sees them, climbing the walls, then tumbling down all around her.

E S
R

H o l
W ag. Slutbitchshedev

Now they scurry around her feet like rats, tripping her up as she moves from room to room. Words made flesh, dissolving into wraiths of letters again so that they slip into her head. They are not like her voices, nothing like that at all. The voices have mostly been kind to her, have spoken pleasantly, as she has spoken to them. These are only words, letters and words, letters making words, words making the letters, round and round and round.

Sometimes, she tries to catch them, grabbing after a B, before it joins to ITC and H; reaching for a W, and an H, and an… but they are gone, further up the wall, or down along the corridor. Sometimes, she cannot read them, until she moves in closer, closer, almost touching, puzzling, mouthing each letter, like a child learning to read. K…I…L… And then she will think, 'no, I do not want to read that. I will not…' and she shakes her arms in front of them, and turns away.

– And yet they are only words.

– And words can never hurt you.

She has heard that before… a long time ago. 'Sticks and stones may break my bones, but words will never hurt me.' A rhyme chanted in childhood. A school-yard retort, when others were name-calling; or said by her mother, when she went home sad, because Emily/Joan/Mary had called her fat/stupid/ugly. If Mother said it, it must be true. And yet… a cut on her knee from a stone hurt, bruised, bled, but then it was gone, with a dab of salve and a kiss. But the words lingered. You could not forget them. They followed you everywhere, just like they are following her now, all through the house.

– I will go out, I must go out, I need food, I will go out and forget, at least for a while. I will go out, and be free of the words.

She dresses in her peacock hat and bright clothes. She will carry hope with her, she will hold her head high.

She goes out of the back door, to avoid the pile of letters on the mat, and walks bravely down the road, one step, two steps, three…

Witch. Trollop. Viper. Monster. Sinner. Bitch.

The words are following behind her, like a dog trotting after her faithfully. She tries to walk faster, but they are still there. She slips into an alleyway, thinking she will watch them pass, but, no, they swerve in behind her, laughing.

Another step, another, her legs growing heavier.

– They are sapping the spring from my step. They are draining the colour from my clothes. And yes, they are there, clinging to her, turning the rainbow hues black. She cannot brush them away.

She turns around and heads back. Home.

The peacock must go again. She takes it to the kitchen table to pluck. One feather, two feathers. Yes, one by one, she drops them on the fire. The eye burnt last, if burning was shrivelling, and dissolving in sepia liquid. Peacock blue turned to oozing rust.

The purple dress must go, too. And the canary yellow. And the scarlet. Their colours are the colours of the flames. Soon, it is hard to tell the cloth and the flame apart. Soon, she has burnt all her new clothes, bought to celebrate her return to life. What can she wear instead? Black, she must go back to black.

Black place, black house, black clothes.

– They are there, in the box, on top of the wardrobe.

Widows' weeds, just like she had worn before. She pays

no attention to the moth holes, and the mildew, the smell of age. And death.

And they fit perfectly, in height and girth, as if they have been made for her. As if they are for her.

That night she thinks the voices have returned. The darkness has called them, perhaps. They will bring her back, as they did before. They will vanquish the sly new words with their strong, vibrant tones. Except… they are not strong, they are not vibrant. They are not grown-up and reassuring. Up and down, up and down they go, trilling, and tralling. Sniggering. High-pitched whispers and giggling. The sound of children. The sound of children's 'fun', another of their silly games, like the sticks and stones.

Grace knew this from before, when she was lost in the darkness – children appearing at her windows, trying her back door. It was what they did, if they thought someone was strange. There was no harm in it… no real harm, in their na-na-na-nahing, and their rattling and knocking. There is no harm in it. But then… you bitch, you slut, spoken in the voices of angels.

She is sure that is what they are saying.

How can they know such things? And why are they saying them to her? As if she is Esther…

– The women. Those harpies in the Square. Their mothers, no doubt. See what bitc… how cruel they are.

– Are they the ones who write the letters? Do they tell their children to do this?

– Shouting the words at you. Making them real.

– The written word, the spoken word, which is worse? To have a word said, or to have it written to you?

'Whore!'

– Ignore them, they are only children.

And suddenly, she is not so sure they are saying the words. Is it no more than their giggling, or the rustling of their boots in the bushes? It makes no difference. The words are with her, anyway, and won't let her alone.

But still, the children are in the front garden, the letters come in the front door. The wind blows from the sea, carrying rumour with it. And the windows on the front are wide, and face three ways. There is a room at the back of the house she has never been in. The door is stuck, and there has been no need.

– The back will be warmer, the back is better protected, the back is safer.

– Try the door again. Push harder.

And she does, and finds herself in a room no more than an arm-span wide, with a narrow, hard bed. Bare, except for a single shell on the bedside table. A razor shell.

– It is airless and dark. Those shutters… There is hardly room to move.

– But you can be hidden away here. You can be safe. There will be no cruel voices. The words can't get in. Listen!

And there is, at that moment, nothing.

She fetches some bedding, and shuts the door.

Scritch-scratch, scritch-scratch. A mouse, that's all it is, behind the skirting. The place is full of them. Or a spider, working its way through the horse-hair in the walls – such thick walls, with their wallpaper and lath-and-plaster and yard-deep stone. Nothing can get in here, can it? And I have plugged the gaps in the window-frame with the pages from the books that I did not burn, and brought more rugs in here, so that there is not a single crack visible, and every night I push the small chair against the door, and check the clasp on the shutters is tight. I am safe here from everything but mice and spiders. And words…

Now I stay here in the day too, on the narrow bed, with the quilt and blankets pulled round me. If need be, I slip down to the kitchen for some bread and cheese, if there is any left after the mice. But I prefer to stay here.

Strange, how I hated it so much at first. I was put in here like a servant, when I should be in my rightful place as the mistress of the house. I should be in the grand front-bedroom, in the four-poster bed, with its carpeted floor and brocade drapes, and… space, light… light from its bay-window, facing left, right and forwards, catching as much sun as there ever could be in this cowering house. A room that, on its own, was as big as any place I had lived in: a bed for two bigger than the one I had shared with four others, brothers and sisters. The marriage bed.

And finally, I was there, walking past his mother, holding my valise that contained all my belongings, smirking inside. Well, in truth, I couldn't stop the smirk reaching my lips, as I mimicked her own upturned mouth that she had shown me all through my early weeks there. True, it had been wiped away through the months of his recovery. She had been quiet then, thinking, perhaps, that familiarity was all that was necessary for Edmund to realise his mistake. But the opposite was true, for here he was, at the end of the summer declaring he was better still. No need for him to stay downstairs any more. At last, we could move into the master-bedroom together, at last we could live as man and wife.

How she must have hated that moment. How it must have nagged at her, and needled her, until she was goaded into action. And more words…

Not the ones of old, not Jezebel, harlot, Delilah, raining down on me from behind the bible. No, she could not risk that, now that he was about again. Quieter now, she littered her conversation with small gibes, challenging my intentions and abilities, questioning my authority – except there was no authority; everything in that house was still ordered by her. It must remain as it was, as it had been since her own marriage, in memory of her dead husband. Our meals were as she dictated at the start of each day, and as I was unable to communicate with the serving-woman or the trades-people, what could I do about it? What could I do about the pig-swill she called 'cowl', or the rabbit stew, rabbit pie, rabbit 'joint'; rabbit, rabbit, rabbit, as if we were still bleedin' well at war! Then there were the three-time daily prayers, the bible-reading, and church-going – all just as she wanted. The purse-strings were in her hands, so that I had no money for my own needs, for my own plans. I could do nothing without money.

I tried. A little word to Edmund, accompanied by my saucer-eyes and fluttering lashes. But it was the one thing he was firm about.

'She is old,' he would say. 'She is my mother.'

'I am your wife,' I could have said back. But I knew that in some things, the act was more than the word.

Ah, yes, the act. The master-bedroom, the marriage-bed, she could have no sway there. Oh, she tried, with her little hints that 'Edmund must not have too much… excitement.' And 'Dr. Pritchard has said there is still much need for caution. You must not over-exert yourself, my dear!' And she would keep him talking downstairs, as bed-time approached, until he would doze off in his chair, and she would put a blanket around him, and say 'better to leave him sleep.'

But no, she could not hope to beat me there.

Yet, it wasn't that I wanted it. I had been glad, almost, of the peace I had been granted those first months – the peace my body had been allowed. My breasts, between my legs, that had existed only for the use and abuse of man, for… how long, now? Since that first… well, however long, those years of pawing, and clawing and mouthing and salivating over… well, they had been mine again; it was *my* body.

But now I must offer it to my husband as being rightfully his, and hope to bind him to me with desire and need, so that she would become as nothing to him – a hindrance, even. And perhaps he would even banish her to another house in the village – ah, the bliss of that.

We managed, somehow. There was fumbling, and some careful positioning on my part, because, after all, his body would always be damaged, and then there was a look on his face that out-did all those other looks of pathetic gratitude. 'Esther, my Esther!' Oh so many 'Esthers' then. 'My love, my darling', 'my darling, my love.' Words I hated as much as harlot, bitch and slut, as they jostled inside me, furring my tongue, making me retch; seeing them as chains binding me, as well as him. And they were words I had heard before, from my father, excuses spluttered between his tears and his drool. So that I had come to prefer the men who took me in silence, and dismissed me at once, with no demands, giving me no reminder of what had gone before. But no, there could be no silence with him, there must be that incessant crooning of my name, my virtues, his devotion.

Still, it was done.

And then, a prayer answered. *My* prayer, not hers, as if God were working for *me*, not for his faithful bleedin' servant! She was gone. Taken by the flu, turning to pneumonia, within a few days. Not the Spanish flu – that would have finished us all, but the usual winter variety. Another lie: 'The coast is such a healthy place to live. The sea air keeps all the germs away.' How I laughed at that, when I heard half the village was down with it. And Edmund caught it, too, with his lungs already weak, and for a day or two I could think 'It will end now, and I will be free, I'll be out of here.' Except, somehow, he recovered – well, after a fashion. It was a step backwards, turned back to how he was before the Spring, and his grief for his mother weakened him further.

Still, at least *she* was gone, carried out of there in an oak coffin, to be laid to rest behind her beloved church. An easy passing... A blameless passing.

'Give her this three times a day,' the doctor told her, handing her Lambert's Asthmatic Balsam. 'Or try some heated elderflower wine. It will help her breathing. And mop her brow with a cold flannel. It will keep her temperature down. And a spoon of broth to keep her strength up.' She stood there, at the door of the sick-room, looking down at the old woman, who looked back, mouthing words. 'Jezebel.' Or was it 'help me!'? She smiled and turned away. 'I have done as you said. I have given her all she needs,' she told him.

Murderer. Killer. Some amongst the letters blamed me for her death – something else to add to my sins. No, I had nothing to do with that. There was no need – she went so quickly. The doctor himself said there was nothing to be done, there was no hope, she was old. See how the letters lie? If they lie about that, can they not lie about anything? Why should anything they say be true? Yes, I was glad. I can't pretend otherwise, though I pretended it then with Edmund, as I pretended so many things. There were tears, even – I was a regular Lilian Gish. But, beneath, my heart was soaring. I could not believe my luck. I would be able to become the mistress of the house now, the path to my escape had become clearer. So, yes, it was what I wanted, but no, I did not lay a finger on her.

Strange, though, I felt almost deprived of victory because she would now not witness it. Still, even if I could not gloat over the flesh, I could work to dirty her memory, and relish that, instead.

It was then that I burnt her bible, while Edmund was still burning in his fever. I had already thrown the precious lectern out the back, laughing as I had hoped to laugh at her, but now it was the turn of the book itself.

'I need to keep the stove going, my dear,' I told him. 'For your broth. For boiling the sheets.'

I sat in the kitchen, feeding the pages into the stove. And I could not help wishing she was looking down at this moment, even though I did not believe, as she did. I smiled, too, from pleasure at the warmth – that her bible was warming me, when she had worked so hard to deprive me of heat, that her words were feeding the flames, not of Hell, but of hearth – my hearth. I saved the leather-bound cover till last, and watched as her family went up in flame and smoke – the family that did not include me, because she had never added that 'm.' followed by my name.

'It is the end of them now,' I thought. 'The end of the Blighs.'

He had told me there were no others; he, the only child, his parents only children, no cousins. No one. No more now. Good riddance, I thought, to her and all of them, to whoever was begat by whoever, who married whichever, and died whenever.

And then, God Almighty, he recovered.

The doctor said there must be an inner strength that his frail and puny body belied, while Edmund babbled about his wonderful nurse, and how love had the power to keep the spirit fighting. Halle-bloody-lujah. I nodded and smiled, as I always nodded and smiled, as I sat beside him, yet again, with my sewing.

'What are you doing, my dear?' he asked.

'Just some repairs,' I said. 'Nothing fancy.'

I had gone through the house, gathering all her handiwork as I found it, anything with 'M.B.' sewn in the corners. Some I put on the fire, after the bible. But I could not burn it all, so I unpicked the tiny stitches one by one, and rubbed away the shadow they left. Then I stitched my own initials in their place. 'E.B.' – far neater, I thought, more cleverly fashioned, declaring my ownership of the piece, the house, and him.

Look. Look. How fine the work is! Still so plain to see, so easy to read. My writing was, of course, so much improved by then. Elegant, curling initials… not so different from the script of the letters, yet worked in thread, not ink. So much harder, in, out, in out, yet so well executed. *E.B.* Esther Bligh, mistress at last.

Still, all this was no more than a stop-gap, to make my insides warm, as the flames of the bible burning made my flesh warm; to make my heart flutter. After all, I had no desire to stay in that house, even if I ruled over it. But at least I had hope; I had a plan. If Edmund wouldn't die, well then I must leave, some way or other, but I needed money to do that, I wanted money, it was my due. Why else had I married him, but to get some comfort in life? With his mother gone I would be in charge of the house-keeping, and yes, I, despite ignorant of my letters, had always been sharp with numbers, seeing them as pounds, shillings and pence, needing to be added and subtracted, and, if I was lucky, multiplied and saved. I would work on Edmund and his bank account, I would sell whatever I could. And then, when I had enough, I would go. Yes, I would have preferred him dead – there would have been more money then, because the house would be mine, mine to sell – and how I would love that moment when I got rid of their precious 'home'. But still, I would make do with the leaving, as long as I had enough money. For yes, that was my due, for the time I had spent in this soul-suffocating fortress, with a fool for company.

Here I am still. The fool was me, not him. I had thought I was so clever, when I lay with him. I had thought I was strengthening my power over him, above *her*. That was all, my only intent. And then she was gone, and I had those few weeks of feeling my way, stretching my authority, planning ahead. I lit fires in every room then – not just the kitchen, or where he lay. True, the house did not fully warm. It had been cold and wet for too many years – cold to its bones, the same as I was. But it was better. And I began my inventory of the valuables of the place. Not near enough as much as I hoped. The porcelain tea-set, so proud on its dresser, was full of secret, spreading cracks. The silver cutlery turned out to be plate. And a woman such as she, one so plain and joyless, did not indulge in jewellery, except for the wedding and engagement rings buried with her (yes, lying in her coffin with her, so that I could not even claim those!). So there were no treasures to be found hidden in little boxes and cubby-holes, small and easy to pawn. Still, I was sure it was simply a question of time and perseverance, and…

… the bleeding. Suddenly, I became aware that there had been no bleeding, this month… or the last. There had been so much going on that I had not thought of it, the first time I missed. But now…

The way I had lived in London… I needed to know such things, where my body was at, what steps needed to be taken. Strange that I was caught before with him, marrying when there was no need. And now, here it was again! I could not believe it! How could I be so unlucky? How could I be such a fool?

Still, there were ways and means, tried and practised many times over. Mind, they had let me down before, until nature had played its dirty trick on me as it was doing again, now. And so it began. The boiling-hot baths – not easy with such plumbing. If the gawping maid was not around, I would resort to the zinc tub in the kitchen – saucepan-fuls from stove to bath. Wearisome work, but I had done it enough times in the past. I wanted pain, then, yearned to feel the wrenching of my insides and then the warmth between my legs. But, no, there was nothing.

Gin. I must try gin. But there was none in the house, the resident widow having been uninclined to ruin, and how could I get it? Oh, how the tongues would be set wagging, if I appeared in the public house, wanting to buy gin. I could not plead it for Edmund – gin was not the invalid's tipple. So, no, I could not use gin, just as I knew there was no-one I could turn to to 'help' me. Of course, there would be someone here, just as there was in the back streets of London. They existed in every place, even one as remote as this. Here, it would be a witch, living in a half-ruined cottage, up on the mountain, or in the wood – if there was a wood. Some old crone, a dried-up, gossipy old woman, like those in the Square gathering her herbs and making her potions. But who exactly, and where exactly, I had no idea.

I tried my own concoctions, filling the house with their smells, so that even Edmund got wind of them. 'I am trying a new medicine for your chest, Edmund, something I read of. I'm afraid it isn't working.' And it didn't. I retched and retched, until there was nothing left inside me – except a baby. The weeks went on. I tried jumping down the stairs, falling, even. How glad I was, then, that the mother had gone. She, no doubt, would have known what I was up to.

There were crueller methods, of course… the needle. There was bleeding, then. But it was the wrong sort, I knew at once. The child kicked in protest in my womb, and burrowed itself tighter.

The child… A child. A brat. Growing inside me, until I could hide it from Edmund no longer. Oh, I tried as long as I could, pretending I was getting fat, taking out all my dresses. But, in the end, I had no choice but to tell him, for I knew the maid would know it soon enough. And the doctor was still calling every week, and the nurse, who had been employed to come every day. And then… the joy. I couldn't believe it, I could not fucking believe it.

'A miracle,' he said. Well yes, that one such as he was capable of fathering a child.

'My wondrous Esther!' As if I had given him all the treasure in the world, or made all his dreams come true. That was what he said, blathering on about his life now being fulfilled, that he, who had been so lucky, to have such a beautiful, caring wife, was now to be fully blessed with a child. Marvellous, beautiful, wonderful, incredible – there was no end to his over-blown outpourings.

And it rallied him again. Something else I could not believe.

'I am determined to be well for the boy, Esther. It will be a boy, I am sure of it. I, we, will have a son. And I will be well enough to be a proper father to him, to do the things a father does with his son. I promise you!' Someone else to collect birds' eggs and shells with, to teach to read, to talk about stones, and seaweed and clouds with. Such a lucky child!

Endlessly he carried on about our future, how wonderful it was going to be, in this perfect house, in this marvellous place. Our wonderful family. Years ahead he planned, years and years stretching out before me.

There was a day when I walked down to the beach again. 'I need some fresh air, Edmund. The sickness, you know.' The sea was its usual grey. I had come to know by then that it was a nonsense to describe it as blue. It was the same with the sky, in this place, at least. 'It is the mountains,' he told me. 'They cast a shadow, and gather the rain to them.' Yes, well, that wasn't what he told me before we got there.

The water weltered towards me. A spring tide. See, I had learnt that from him – that the sea was high, now, and it was nothing to do with the season, but the state of the moon. How lucky I was to have been given this knowledge by him, and all else he had given me besides. So much to be thankful for… I took a step closer to the waves.

It was just a moment. It was not for me.

But what was for me? A child. A husband. In this place. How could I endure it? How could I possibly survive?

I prayed. I prayed, I suppose, to the Devil that he would end it. A miscarriage, like before, was it too much to ask?

And I still tried the various ways, even in the knowledge that it became more dangerous with every week that passed. I did not care. And if I succeeded, well, surely the grief would finish him off, so that I would be free – two birds with one stone, you might say. But each attempt I made was answered by another frantic kicking from within. 'Edmund is right,' I thought. 'It must be a boy. Another man abusing my body, making use of it for his own ends.' Already, I could not believe what he had done to me. I would stand naked in front of the mirror, and gaze on my bloated stomach, cradle my hands round my aching breasts, see the life sapped from my hair, feel the spirit draining from me. That I had come to this…

Yet all *this* turned out to be nothing compared with the birth. Oh, how he punished me then, this boy, this 'perfect baby boy' – that was how they introduced him to me as I lay there half dead after the hours of birthing, the fight we had endured. It was as if he knew, knew that it was safer to stay inside. But out he came in the end, pulled, pushed, coaxed, threatened. And breathed. And cried. And lived.

Mother. Another word from the letters. Another word from before. I had one, once, for all the good it did me. And then, when I came here, another was dumped upon me. And now I had somehow become one… But it was something I could never be. The letters made it plain, and it was something they spoke the truth about. 'What kind of mother are you?' they said. 'How can any mother do that?' 'You do not deserve the name of "mother"!' Well, I hadn't asked for it. I didn't want it. I hated every moment of it, whatever the doctor, the midwife, and Edmund – most of all Edmund – thought, with his 'you will be so wonderful, such a caring mother, just as you are so caring to me!' I, who could hardly bear to enter his room now that there were other warm spaces for me; I, who let the nurse attend to his needs whenever she was there; I, whose skin puckered and squirmed at his touch, and insides spewed at his words.

That moment they put the child in my arms, when my face was supposed to light up in adoration despite my weakness and pain, when all my former anguish was supposed to dissolve into love – well, it didn't bloody happen; nothing changed at all, not a thing. I still simply wanted it to go away. Did the doctor see it, and the midwife, with her shifting eyes and flapping ears? Because for once I had no energy for play-acting, and I found myself glad Edmund was not there, until I remembered how blinded he was by his foolish passion.

Still, he came soon enough, and oh, the ecstasy! That it was a boy… 'My boy, my son, my Esther, my darling, my baby, my son'. Until his words were lost in the tears he shed, as he held the child, making the doctor banish him again, afraid of effect on his nerves, afraid that it might kill him.

And I was glad, then, of my own weakness, that I was deemed too frail in those first few weeks, to look after it, so a wet nurse was brought in. Thank God for that – why should I want anything to do with a crying, squalling, messing creature? Why should I have any pleasure in that? I was simply not born to be a mother. What is so wrong in that?

The child was puny, sickly at the start, no wonder, perhaps, considering what it had been through in the womb. Yet all too soon he began to grow stronger. The nurse was doing her job well, Dr. Pritchard told me. But a thriving, blooming brat was not what I wanted. I told the woman I was feeling better, so there was no further need of her. I wanted her gone, I wanted to be alone with the child, to…

I did not know what I wanted, or what I was thinking. I swear I had no plan just then.

Of course, Edmund was there. But he was lost in his land of make-believe, with his fairy princess and his son, the prince, Edmund the second; the land where they all lived happily ever after, for ever and ever.

He did not notice that the weight the baby had gained was lost again. The doctor saw it, of course, frowned over him, prodded him here, pinched him there, asked if he were feeding well.

'Yes,' I said. 'Yes, he is fine.'

She sat there, with the child in her arms, looking at it. 'It' was what she called him, when no-one else was there. Strange, how it would nuzzle close to her, when she had never fed it on the breast. Stranger, still, how it would look at her, the same way as his father, needing, wanting, always asking something of her that she could not give, until she could stand it no longer. She would lay it back down, then, and the crying would begin. 'Colic,' she told him. 'He has eaten too much, too fast. That is all.'

He was there; he was gone. He was christened; he was buried. It was not so strange, with the men coming back from the war unmanned, and the Spanish flu, and the other flu, and the eternal bitter, damp air of this place, even in summer time. It was not so strange, besides – there were always babies who died amongst those who lived. More, surely.

LIAR.

LIAR

'Liar' written in capitals, yelling from half the page. LIAR inside my head.

Lies. All lies. There was no pillow, there was no poison slipped into his milk. No 'accidental' fall. A chill, nothing else, that his frail body could not fight. That was all.

They took him in a box to the graveyard where his unknown grandmother lay and all his ancestors lay. I thought 'It will finish Edmund now,' as he leaned against me, thinking to support me, when it was I who must stop him throwing himself into the hole after the coffin. I thought 'It is better this way. He should never have existed. He was a mistake, and mistakes must be put right.' I thought lots of things, but I did not think of the child.

Oh, what doom was called down upon us now. Whatever gloom I had thought reigned over the house, it was nothing to the despair that engulfed our 'family' after the death of 'our beloved son'. That's on his gravestone. That's what he was in Edmund's constant mewling. The curtains must be kept drawn at all times, and the morbid clothes not long forsaken in our mourning for his mother must be put on again, without respite, and, since we could not possibly have appetites, on account of our grief, our meals must be reduced to bread and water, and, and, and – whatever misery could be thought up, so must we embrace it, so that the days when his mother ruled the roost began to seem almost cheerful by compare! Our little excursions to the beach or the mountain were remembered as pleasant interludes! Edmund was returned to his bed almost permanently now, and I was not to leave the house, because why should I want to, when I was so sad?

There was one place I could go. I was allowed, encouraged even, to visit the little grave. 'Take flowers for him, Esther. Sit with him. Tell him how we love him. Tell him I am sorry I cannot visit.' As if this bloody life-sucking child still existed and must be spoken to, when all I had wanted was that he cease to be.

So off I would go, black except for a small white circle of face, and make my way passed the harridans in the Square, up to behind the church, on the slope of the mountain. Strange how the women looked at me differently, then, nodding towards me, with no hands raised to their mouths, a doleful look in their eyes. Pity. I knew it for pity, thinking, as they did, with my baby dead, even one such as I deserved sympathy for that. Was I supposed to be grateful for that? Was I supposed to return their nodding, approach them, even, and thank them for their condolences?

Pity – something I hate as much as hurt, more, perhaps. That anyone should think I needed pity, wanted it, when there were so many more desirable things in life. Such as the things I wanted from Edmund when I met him. Money, jewels, clothes, material goods, not his 'Poor, poor Esther', not his watery eyes. And certainly not his child.

So I would sit by its grave, looking out across the sea. 'Not a bad place to be laid to rest,' Edmund had said when his mother died. He was right, I suppose, if one liked the sea and the sky, if one believed that the spirit still lived, hovering above, able to enjoy a view, able to see it through the perpetual gloom that enveloped the place. And it was almost pleasant to me, then, not because I liked that scenery, but because at least I had some peace from my husband's constant wailing. And the baby was in his box, safe, hidden away at my feet, a good place for him to be. Out of harm's way, out of my way. What was wrong in that?

One day, when I got up from my vigil, instead of heading straight back, I turned upwards and begun to climb the path at the side of the graveyard, on towards the heights. I had been here once or twice with Edmund, on his 'educational forays', as he called them. I thought, now as then, that by climbing I would finally reach a point above it all. And yes, there was a place, with a large stone conveniently fallen, where you could look down on the entire village. For once it was a clear day, and I could see how it was hemmed in on both sides, by the sheer cliff to the right and the long headland to the left. And the sea, always the sea, stretching all the way, to… I still didn't know where. No doubt I had been told by Edmund, but had not listened, as I didn't listen to so many things… things that had no meaning for me.

Beneath me, little grey boxes cowered together, sheltering their little grey minds within. The ominous cliff marked our house, and yes, for a moment, I thought 'our'. It was where I lived with Edmund, my husband. But it was not mine. It never had been, it never would be; for, if I ever came to own it, I would get rid of it straight away. More than ever now, I knew I did not belong in it, just as I had never belonged in this place.

I carried on walking up the mountain. 'I will come to the top,' I thought. 'I will breathe there. I will open my lungs, I will shout, and throw my arms wide.' Perhaps I could even dance… But there was no top. What I had thought was the summit, was simply a ridge, that dipped down, then rose again to another ridge. And another, another, another, until the ridges became peaks far higher than where I stood, pleated against each other, struggling to be tallest, on, as far as I could see, on, into eternity. And I could not breathe, or shout, because I was out of breath with the climb. And I could not breathe, because the jagged crests were like barbed wire put there to keep prisoners in.

And I could not breathe because there was nowhere for me to go but back.

And still there is nothing when Grace wakes from the deepest sleep since she came here. No wind or rain or trundle of the sea on the pebbles; no hissing and garbling from the children. Not even a voice... anyone's voice. Today – if it is day, because this room is dark – for once, she is alone. And she is hungry. She wants to eat, something else she can hardly remember. Perhaps it has all been a bad dream. Perhaps it will all be different today.

And yes, the landing window is a vague strip of blue, and the dust of the house dances in sun-beams.

But when she reaches the hall, there on the mat is the pile of letters. Mrs Esther Bligh, Mrs Esther Bligh, Mrs Esther Bligh.

Still, what are they, but scraps of scored paper? Does she know if *any* of it is true? She doesn't even know who is alive and dead. Just because Edmund's name was scratched out on a book, it doesn't have to mean anything. And what sign of a baby has she come across in this house? No carefully worked lace robes and cot-covers amongst the linen, no likeness, or lock of hair. She should have questioned Mrs Evans further, instead of being silenced by a single look. But she can't ask again. But who else can help her?

Who? Or what? There is somewhere that can tell such things. And the day is so fine...

The graveyard lies against the mountain behind the church. The dead are caught between the high ground and the deep sea. The space is cut in four by a well-worn path, with a bench at the cross-roads, a perfect place for watching the view and the graves and to catch your breath after the steep slope. Today, the sea and sky merge in blueness: it is beautiful, the first beauty she has seen since coming here. A good place to be buried, if there is such a thing, if one has to die. Better, certainly, than the cemetery where her mother lay beside her father, where she had gone every day, unable to say goodbye, until she had met John. Still, it is too cold to sit for long, so she gets up and wanders among the stones just below her. The prime site, Grace guesses – not too far from the church, not too far to walk, yet still having that view. The plots for the rich of the town, perhaps.

And there is the name, 'BLIGH', carved in marble, painted in gold, the chosen monument of a wealthy man, dated from more than a century ago. Then she sees another and another: all Blighs, husbands, wives, fathers/mothers … all gathered together, fanning out from the centre clearing, their grave-markers getting fewer and poorer as the years move closer. Marble, then stone. Wood? Does anyone have wood any more? Not here… And finally, close to the path, but further along, she finds Edmund Bligh, 'Captain Edmund Bligh, beloved husband of Esther, died 1923.' Beloved.

'Perhaps, after all, the story told by the letters is untrue; everything I have come to believe is nonsense.'

'Liar. Hypocrite'

And where is she, where is Edmund's loving wife? Not next to him – the grave there is tiny, as is the stone, to stop it drowning in shadow. Grace kneels down on the hard ground to see the inscription. Another Edmund, dead at only a few months old. Dead, just a year or so before his father. Beloved son, now, of Edmund and Esther.

She traces the lines of the names with her finger, then runs her hand over the mound. The grave of a child is such a small thing, but it is still a thing. She had no grave for her child; some would say she had no child. To her, it had existed since she was old enough to imagine a future, for all she wanted was to be a wife and mother, the guiding light of a perfect family. Just as Mother had been to her. Two children, a boy and a girl. No, four, two boys and two girls, alternating in age. Yes, four! Four, so that they would always have someone to play with, so that they would never be alone, as she was. And when she met John, it was the start of the dream coming true, because *he* talked of it too, down there on the front, hidden by the church roof, on a day as perfect as this. Then it happened, she knew it from the moment of conception. And those few days and few weeks, when she believed John would come home safe and sound to find her waiting with her – their – baby, were the happiest of her life. Then he and it were gone. A bloody mess on her bed-sheets, that she scooped together and burnt outside. So there was no body, and no grave. Nothing. Nowhere for her to come and sit, nothing to care for. Even Esther had had that – if she wanted it.

There was no grave for John, either. Lost, missing in action, the man who came to the door said. Some were found later and brought home, he offered, trying to stop this woman's breath-jerking sobbing. Maybe it was possible that would happen with John… But no. How awful it was to imagine there could be no body. Those few nights when he was asleep beside her, she would put her hand on his chest and feel the beat of his heart, and the rise of his breath, the gloss of his skin, the firmness of his muscles. He would come back, of course he would come back, someone so full of life couldn't die. Then he was gone. Not even a scrap of flesh awash in blood. Evaporated in the gas, perhaps, rising in the air, wandering the heavens until his voice reached her again. Still insubstantial… but something, better than *nothing*.

Esther could not have killed her husband; and no mother could kill her child. It was all a terrible mistake, based on malicious gossip. Was it the writer of the letters who was evil, tormenting a poor widow, a bereft mother? Beloved.

But why isn't she buried next to them? Because the grave next to them is that of 'Maud', wife of Arthur, mother of Edmund. There is no sign of Esther at all.

She struggles up and wanders among the stones, searching. On some, she has to scrape the lichen away to make the words out. Age has worn the letters to no more than feeble lines and suggestions. Others are plain. Davies, Evans, Jones again and again. The more recent include soldiers from the war: fresh flowers lie on them, they are well-tended. This is what she would have done for John, if she had had him back. If only she had had him back…

Names rise up from the stones. Dav/Evans/Bli. She doesn't want this, she wants to keep the silence as long as she can. She doesn't want it to be like it is in the house, or when the words followed her down the street. But here they are. Names, numbers, dead, all dead. John. John is there. Not him, of course it is not him. It is not John Marlowe, her John. It is John Richards. John, James, Mary. Another John, a baby 'John' , yes, she had even named the child, who was no more than a whisper. It would be a boy, of course. John would want the first to be a boy. He would come home to a son, his heir, to carry on his line, as the baby Edmund should have done. BORN/SON OF/Daughter of… Died… She doesn't want this. DIED. 18/19. 1902, 1918, 1945. DEAD OF… Not now.

Grace wants to keep the sun and the blue sky and the fresh air longer. She wants the sounds to stay at bay, but she must leave the names and the numbers and the dead. She must go now. There beside her is a gate in the wall, with a path leading from it, upwards. She will walk higher up the mountains. Why not? She has never been there, there has somehow been no time, and with the weather always so bad it is not a good idea to go wandering on the heights. Most days, she hasn't even been able to see them. Today is different. Today everything seems to be different, with the sunshine, and a quiet dead for company. The view from up there will be wonderful – perhaps she will see all the way to Ireland, if Ireland is that way. She is not really sure. The village will be no more than a child's toy-town to her, where there can be nothing to be frightened of. If she climbs up there, perhaps she will be able to breathe in the fresh mountain air, to fill her lungs with it, stretching her arms wide. Perhaps she will feel free.

At the upper end of the churchyard wall there is a small enclosure, a pauper's cemetery, she supposes. No more than a few misshapen graves lost amongst brambles and long, matted grass. Some are marked with plain wooden crosses, rotting now, most of them. There is one at the very top, apart from the others. Grace pulls at the weeds surrounding it, then scrapes at the creeping moss. ES she sees. ER. – LIGH. Letters making words again. A name. A name she knows is Esther Bligh. But Esther was not a pauper. There are other people who are not allowed to lie with the baptised dead, Grace knows. Those who take their own lives: some churches will not allow them inside holy ground. Or those who have committed the worst of the sins, broken the sixth commandment: 'Thou shalt not kill'.

She turns back down the path, running, stumbling as she goes. She will not walk up the mountain now, she will not go anywhere but 'home'. She hates that she must call it that, but where else is there for her to go?

– Where have you been?
– Where were you?
– What were you doing?

As soon as she steps through the door, it is there, though she had been so quiet with the key, the handle, her steps.

– I… Just…

– Don't think I don't know. And don't think I don't know you. You think you are different from me. You think you are better than me.

– I know who you are.

– I am—

– I know what you are… Liar. Hypocrite. You killed your child, too, didn't you?

NO!

But she did, didn't she? If she hadn't grieved so much for John, if she hadn't cried so much, if she had thought of the baby that she knew was inside her.

– I should have put it first. I should have remained strong for the child. It is what John would have wanted for me, to be brave, to stop my tears and think, instead, that I would have this child – his son – so that something would remain of him. Never mind that there was no body, no grave: there would be the greatest thing of all. A child. But I was selfish.

I gave in to my grief. It was what *I* wanted to do. So I lost John *and* the child. And if he had lived, the son I knew I was going to have, well, I wouldn't have been alone, I would have had someone to love, and to love me… Instead…

– Yes, instead, what have you got, but this? And me.

Now the dead follow her up the stairs as she goes to the only place that is left for her. She hasn't left them in the churchyard, after all. All the Davieses, and Joneses, and Evanses, and the Blighs, and the soldiers and the mothers and the fathers and sons and daughters of. And John. And the baby. They climb with her, along with the words, CHILD KILLER, MURDERER.

– Me, yes, me…

She creeps inside, and once again, shuts the door.

It is harder than ever to breathe now. Shut up in this little room, with all its cracks and crannies stuffed with rags and rugs to keep the words at bay. But air is finer than letters, surely, it will sneak in between the threads or through the splinters of wood. And yet, and yet… there are days when my mouth gapes desperately, and the weight on my chest grows heavier, and the walls get closer, and then I know that this place will be my coffin. I will be shut up forever, back where I began. Soon, soon.

Soon, but not yet. There was indeed a short time when I ruled inviolate over every inch of this house, supreme and unchallenged. The brief interlude I savoured after the loss of his mother had been quickly dimmed by the knowledge of my pregnancy and the birth of the child, and, of course, the pretence of grief after its death governed all other actions, when I had to spend my days keening, sitting at his side soothing his fevered brow, and mopping his tears.

He will die, quickly now, I thought, this will see him off. The doctor thought it, too.

'He is greatly weakened by the shock and the grief,' he told me. 'And his lungs after that last bout are even more fragile.'

He hung on.

Good for nothing, not even death, I thought. 'How marvellous,' I told the doctor, whose amazement was equal to my own.

Still, he did no more than lie there, and there must be someone to rally, and take command, and see to basic, day-to-day practicalities. So, of course, that person must be me.

I went back to my burning and my sewing, continuing my efforts to drive every last memory of 'dear mother' from the place. That was when I ordered the trees to be cut down. I told him after it was done, though, of course, he had heard the noise.

'More light,' I said. 'We need more light. The dark contributes to the damp. And the wood will feed the fires for a good while. You must have fires, you must have warmth.'

'The rooks,' he whispered.

What I wanted to say then, I kept to myself, merely telling him to ssshh, and save his precious breath. 'The rooks are fine,' I said.

'I watched the black birds, as the workmen began to climb. They rose from their nests, with their usual yacking cries magnified ten times, and circled this way then the other, darting forward, then away. I watched, and clapped my hands in glee, as they took one final turn, then broke into haphazard ones and twos, and wheeled away.' She was glad they were gone. She had seen them watching her. They could see all she did. 'It was your fault,' she told him. 'You told me they could talk. I couldn't have that. Or was that something else you lied about? Yes, your fault, again...'

Yes, there was more light then, with the trees gone, except the rain came straight off the sea and hit the windows with greater force, and the gales blew straight at us, instead of sifting through branches first. So that the damp and cold inside were greater, not less.

Now I could see the water without interruption, and the cliff to the side, and the long headland the other way; so that I was constantly reminded of how I was caught here, unable to walk away.

Money, I needed money. It was owed to me.

It was still my plan to leave – what else? – but I would not do it without some money in my pocket. But from where?

There was another book his mother had attended to each Friday evening, poring over it, almost as much as she did the bible. I had seen her working at the kitchen table, curling her arm tight around the book whenever I approached, locking it afterwards in some secret location away from her 'daughter's' prying eye: her housekeeping ledger, her list of accounts, in which every item of expenditure was etched in a column of red, against a column of black incomings. The repository of the family's riches, I thought, my salvation! Imagine, then, my disbelief, when I finally found it, breaking the lock on her desk drawer, opening it in triumph, to see… page after page of empty space beneath 'Monies Received'.

0.00; 0.00; 0.00. Nothing! Nothing at all!

Liar. Thief. Fraud! All these words put on me!

'There is money,' he told me. But did he? The photograph of the house was shown, yet when I scratched my head in desperate recollection, there was no mention of riches. Yes, he gave me money for new things, but that was from his army pay while he went without. There was none of that now. Before that, what had he earned with his book-writing and his studying and his knowledge? Sweet Fanny Adams! So much for books, and learning. Where did they get you? Nowhere.

The household treasures I had thought to sell, that I felt sure must be about here somewhere, if I only had time to look – they had disappeared a long time ago. A silver tea-set, a list of jewellery, china ornaments, they were all here in the book, carefully itemized with the amount received from each sale. Where had the money gone to, besides the little spent on food and clothing? Him! Before the war, it was for this trip, that trip, that lecture. Since – oh, the pounds lost here – his doctor's bills. Each visit, each medicine, more pounds, shillings and pence added, until…

Until…? Of course, I did not know. The entries had finished with her illness. Then, there had been her funeral, the baby's birth, its illness, its funeral, the two of them getting the very best of burials, at Edmund's behest; and Edmund getting worse, and needing more treatment, until…

What was left for me? Nothing, it seemed, as I searched the house from top to bottom, looking in every cupboard, every drawer, every box, for anything of value, again and again. Empty, all empty, except for his books! Row after row of useless words wrapped in paper, with a picture now and then. Good for nothing, like him. Fit for nothing but burning!

'Money,' I said to him. 'I need money, to pay the maid, for food, for the doctor.'

He looked at me, as if he did not understand the question. 'Mother,' he said, as he had said in the past – his answer for everything.

'Your mother is dead,' I reminded him. 'May God rest her soul,' I added, remembering the Hell fire she had wished on me.

'My father,' he said, before losing his words in an outburst of coughing.

There was something, it appeared. A small allowance paid each month from his father's estate, or some such thing, when once his mother had died. I did not understand the terms, but I understood the money. There was enough for food and clothing, if we were careful. And that was all. For richer, for poorer. I had signed up for the former, but it seemed that the latter was to be my lot. To have and to hold. Hold, keep, chain. Holding so tight that you want to scream, but you cannot scream, because your lungs have no air. So that all you want is to rid yourself of those chains. To be free again. To live again.

Thief. They called me a thief. They lied! Yes, I had been one, once, but how would they know that? How would they know that I slipped my hand in a punter's pocket, to reach his wallet, to make more than the pathetic wage he would pay me? Yes, I would have been one still, if there was anything left to steal. Except… there was nothing there. Not a thief, at all, no matter what the words say.

It is warm here. Or warmer, at least.

It is warm, because there is so little air.

She came to this place to breathe again, to bathe in light again, and yet, here she is, smothered in brooding, cloying fug.

Still…

…Still, it is quiet, here. Sometimes. Sometimes quiet enough to hear her own breath, listening for it, as she did once before. It is clearer now, louder, because she has to open her lungs wide, her mouth wide, to reach for any air that is in the room. Only it is not air. Air purifies, opens, invigorates. What surrounds her here is thick with dust and must. Dust, the scrapings of human skin. Who is she breathing in?

She knows.

She knows other things, too. Edmund Bligh knew what it was like to struggle for breath. First, with the gas, then with the illness, and then, finally, when the pillow was brought down over his face.

Pillow. She has read that word so many times. She had laid her head, where that pillow lay. Pillow – a soft, desirable cushion to rest on, to sleep. Not a bad word, at all. Edmund would have been glad of the comfort of pillows after the trenches, glad to rest his aching body. Until…

'Feather beds should be made of domestic birds' feathers, such as geese, duck and fowls. Wild fowl feathers should not be mixed with these feathers, for otherwise, the sick will die hard, and thus the agony of their last moments will be prolonged.'

Where has she heard that? An old wives' tale, nothing else. From an old wife?

But he didn't die from the sickness, did he?

What was it like? Was the suffocation of a pillow different from the gas? Was it easier? What is it like? She holds her pillow over her face. The dark grows darker still. The dips and contours of her bones are filled in. Her hands knead the feathers deeper. She feels them beneath her fingers, sharp. Goose? Duck? Or from some distant mountain lake? Or a cormorant, or gull.

– Take it away, not yet, not yet.

– Yes.

She must get rid of the pillow. Something more to burn, something more to go up in flames and smoke, like she should have done to the letters. It always came back to the letters. The first letter, first. If only she had burnt it, but she didn't, she hadn't. Then the others.

No, no. That isn't her. She has done nothing.

But how does she know about the gas? How does she know about the illness? And yet she does. She knows lots of things. She knows too much. It is there, inside her head now. She sees it all.

There is Esther standing beneath the last remaining pine, dropping feathers onto a garden bonfire. White snow dissolved around her, or escaped into the heavens, to search out the live birds and press themselves to their plumage, yearning to fly again.

Little birds, trying to escape feather by feather, trying to fly away, but falling back into the flames… burning, melting to nothing.

He taught her about the birds, thinking she might love them, but all she did was envy them, being able to fly away across the sea.

He taught her other things, too. Shells, clouds, flowers. 'Pretty', she thought, sometimes, liking the colours, the shapes that made her think 'that is how a flower should be.' But he would smother them in words, squeezing the life out of their beauty. Petals/sepals/cirrus/cumulus. Words she did not understand, that she did not want to understand. Book words.

The books burned in a different way. That is something she learned – things burned differently. Strange, she thought. The hard spine that she expected to linger flared and was gone. Animal, she remembered, glue from the flesh of a horse. The covers… yes, they took their time, thick, meshed paper on leather, that she could not tear, that she must put on whole; their titles blazoned up at her, gold through gold. The titles he had thrown at her, as if she should know them, she must know them – 'classics/the definitive work on/never-bettered'… She liked to see them withering away. The pages would eat into themselves (the eternal damp, perhaps?) So they would hesitate before her, as if to echo his 'look, look.' Look at me. At the rose. At the ammonite. At the humming-bird. The humming-bird, finally rising up in the flames, indigo and scarlet together, pausing a moment, as they did against the nectar, emerald, amber, up, up…

Birds, again. Birds flying again. Escaping again.

The words never flew away, the words in the books, the words in the letters. She thought they did, she thought they turned to ash, or drifted with the smoke, high above the fire. She thought she was saying goodbye to them. But no… the smoke rose, then twisted around, coming back down towards her, so that she breathed it in. She breathed the words in. Bitch, slut, whore. Murderer. No matter how she coughed, and retched, it was still there, stuck in her throat, her gizzard, her head. Did she have a gizzard, or was that just birds…?

Gloves, that she wore as if another layer between his face, the pillow, and her hands would distance the act. Her dress, as if it had borne witness. Those, she put on the coals, too, foolishly throwing the heavy garment in one go, so that it quenched the embers beneath it, so that she must start again. She cut it into sable ribbons, that she dangled one by one, into the heat's core. So many things to burn, for no reason.

Sometimes, for no more reason than that she loves the fire. She has always loved it… since *then*. She loves to stand there and watch it, and feed it, nurture it – that is what you have to do. You must treat it with love; you must feed it your hate. That is what she did before, that is what she does now, standing beneath the sole pine tree, dropping her hate into the flames with care and concern. Oh, how she despairs when the flame fails – worse, when she cannot even ignite it, watching the glowing end of the taper kiss the pages she has laid there so precisely beneath a wigwam of small sticks, only to see the puckered lips back away, like a reluctant lover.

How she loves it, when it takes hold and flares and the flames leap in front of her, so strong that she must step back, fearful for her hair, her loose sleeves. Yet still glad for what she sees. The colour, the heat, and then, the consumption of her offering. Gone. Recompense for what she had not seen… before.

Before.

Time went on, as it does. I got rid of the skivvy, who gargled vengeful words at me – what they were, I had no bleedin' idea. I told the doctor that Edmund was much better, so there was no need for him to call every week. I would contact him, if there was an emergency.

Or death. Death would come first. He was not better. He would surely not last much longer, I thought. He lay there, day after day, hardly moving, his breath no more than a strained wheeze. Looking at me with those eyes whenever I entered the room, whenever I sat by him. He would take my hand then and, if he had any breath for speech, would talk of the child. Of his misery, of my misery. Poor, poor Esther.

Weeks eked out into months, all the same, when all I could hope for was that he would die. Except, yet again, he didn't. Yet again, there he was, whispering 'I will get better for you. I will be stronger for you. Esther. My Esther.'

And he did, and he was. Not fit, not healthy, hardly able to get up from that bed, but breathing stronger every day, eating more every day. Asking for his books to be brought for him, joyful that we would soon be able to resume our studies together. Our shared minds together. Together, always together, here, in our precious home.

No. One of the shortest words. A simple word, yet so full of meaning.

No. A word so often forgone, when it should be said. 'Will you marry me?' No. 'Do you take this man…?' No. 'Will you look after him in sickness and health?' No.

'No' should have been said at the very start. No was said

now to myself. No, I will not put up with this, I will not live this life, which is no life. No.

Winter came again, as bad as the first I had endured on coming here. Winter came, if winter had ever gone. How many fine days had there been since that arrival? How much rain, and cold, and wind had beaten against this place in that time?

'Exceptional,' he mouthed. 'A bad few years. Sorry.' So many fucking sorrys…

And the cold and the wet spread into his lungs again, so that his endless hawking was the accompaniment of our long days. But still he would not die.

The coughing loud, the breathing shallow; the rasping and grasping for air that was not there. I kept the fire lit. I would be warm, why should I not have warmth, when I had so little else? I had the wood from the trees for fuel, so I would keep the flames burning as long as I could, ignoring his fever, the sweat bubbling from his flesh.

I began to talk, then. I was supposed to read to him, and I did at first, but, soon, I would lay the book aside, and let my thoughts scramble pell-mell out of my mouth. I could stop it no longer.

I told him, then, about his mother, of the things she said to me, and how I hated her.

'I burned her bible,' I said, 'I burned the words she called me. I watched your family go up in flames. I laughed.'

'This place,' I said. 'Look! Do you remember?' I took a framed photograph from the wall – the same view as in the post-card he showed me when we met. '"Beautiful," you said. "Wonderful!"'

I smashed the picture on the hearth, then threw it on the fire. 'Hell,' I told him. 'A shit-hole, like this whole bleedin' country,' I said, relishing the thick, joyous freedom of vulgarity on my tongue, saying it again. 'Shit, nothing but shit, like the people who live in it.'

'And her… this house… Home. You said it would be my home, when all it has been is my prison. My fucking prison.'

That will be enough, I thought, he will hate me now. That was what I wanted. If he hates me, all hope will be gone. The future will be gone. And he will wither away and die in despair.

If he hates me, I thought, that cringing look of pity and love will be wiped off his face. I will not have to flounder in his gushing eyes any more.

It was no good, no matter what I told him. Yes, there was puzzlement, a kind of bemusement, as if there was something wrong with… *me. Me!* As if, perhaps, I had caught his fever, and ranted in my delirium; or, as if my grief for the child had unhinged me; or as if someone else was speaking through me… But… there was still love! There was still pity!

'Poor Esther,' his eyes said, 'how I love you and pity you.' The same as it had always been, as if he were speaking to a child, who knew no better.

'Do you think I love you?' I said, as if in reply. 'Do you think I married you for love? I married you, because I thought you were rich, I thought I could get something from you. And because I was carrying a child, someone else's child. I despise you. I despise you, and all your nonsense that you think, somehow, is worthy. Your books, your birds, your flowers, your rocks. Your 'learning', your 'knowledge'. I hate them all. Wait… See…'

I picked up one of his precious books – the most precious to him, I knew – and crossed to the fire with it.

'This is what I've been doing while you lay here. Look! Look! As you were always telling me, as if that was what I wanted to do. Look at what you were showing me. Take pleasure in all those pictures of birds, animals, flowers, as if I would care about such things. Look!'

No careful unstitching then. A swift, harsh rip, tearing the humming-bird in two. Then a casual toss of my arm, to send it sailing into the flames.

'See the pretty colours. Watch its exquisite plumage burn.'

There were tears, then. I swear there were tears for a piece of paper with a drawing on it. But still there was pity floating in their depths, pity for me. Love for me. How could anyone be so forgiving? I could not understand it, except to think he was a fool. An idiot and a fool.

'A pathetic example of a man. That you should still love me, after all I have said and done. A snivelling, cowardly, unnatural human-being. You should have died in France.'

But he hadn't, and still he didn't. He hung on all through another year. Somehow, he hung on to some fine, spun-metal thread of life deep within him. Somehow, he would not die.

How? Another small word. A small question… Another way I liked to spend my time, then. If I were to kill him, how would I do it? Just idle thoughts, nothing else.

In the rooms, in the back streets of London, the girls had talked of arsenic. 'The wife's way,' they called it. 'Easy to get hold of. A little now and then,' they said. This poison, that poison. So easy… His medicines lay on the table beside me – the Horehound Balsam, Lamplough's Saline, the tinctures, mixtures, and extracts, bottle after bottle. His water. All I need do…

The razor. The razor so like the shell that still lay on the table of the little room. Not the neck, no pretence of shaving. No, it would be his wrists. One quick cut on each. A fine, red line, like the line on my finger. There! There! 'I had just slipped out for a moment, Doctor Pritchard. I thought he would be all right. I thought he was better in spirit!'

Blood. There would be blood. Not the single drop that had welled from my hand, but the blood of all his arteries drained out on to the bed. Red. My favourite colour become this. I didn't want that for red. I didn't want him to steal that from me, too.

In truth, I knew it from the start. If I were to do it, I knew how it would be; if… if… but these were just thoughts, just a way to spend my time, as I sat there. Just something to make me feel… better; to make me feel that there may be some end to it. That was all. Still, if I were to do it… ahhh!

Yes. There was a rightness to it, in so many ways.

That the birds would take him, the birds he had loved so much would put an end to him. The birds that he had forced down my throat would be forced into his.

He would have no air! He had little enough as it was, it was something he was used to. Would it be so hard to have the last gasp taken away? A minute or two, surely no more, and then— Cleaner than the gas, softer than the bronchitis, the pneumonia. Easier, easy on him.

Yes.

Yes, till death do us part.

Yes. Maybe. Perhaps. Eeny, meeny, miny… I sat there doing nothing, unable to decide. Rock, paper, scissors – something else from childhood – changed into this.

Later, the letters, too, could not make up their minds. Some would talk of poisoning, borrowing tales from penny dreadfuls. That favourite, arsenic! One, that I had pushed him down the stairs. Stairs! By then, he could not reach the stairs, he could barely get up to piss (oh the joy in that: truly 'in sickness' then!) Stairs – yes, no more than a trip, a slip would have been needed, to break his bird-bones to bits. So easy. But no, I could not use the stairs. A knife, a scarf round his neck – all these were mentioned.

Others confused the timing, saying I killed him just after I killed the baby. Or before, even. Fucking idiots! What did they know?

What do I know?

What did I do?

She sees all these things. So many things.

Now she sees Esther, pulling the pillow from beneath Edmund's head. 'It is better for him to lie flat,' the doctor told her. 'It relieves the pressure on his lungs.' Or was it that he should sit higher? Still…

The pillow is to hide his face, that is all. To hide those eyes, and the way they look at her. To put an end to the pity and the love.

'It will be easier for you, you will be able to rest. You will be with your mother, and the men you left in France, and your son. You will be together again. It is what you want.'

Still she does nothing. She stands there, cradling the pillow, smoothing the cotton slip. It is harder than she thought. Until he whispers, 'Esther… Poor, poor Esther.' So that, finally, she brings the pillow down onto his face.

Again, it is harder than she thought.

'It will be done in a moment,' she tells herself. 'No more.'

'He will feel nothing; I will feel nothing,' she supposes, and presses harder, deeper. Deep down to beyond the cushioning feathers, so that she must feel the sockets of his eyes, the rise of his nose. His gasping lips. She must touch those, and push the pillow between them, so that the feathers are tight, tight within that mouth, the nostrils. Push, and press, with all her might. Then his body begins to buck, and thrash, and shudder beneath the thin coverlet.

'Is he fighting?' she wonders. 'Weak, pathetic Edmund Bligh?'

But no, his arms flail with the rest of him, never reaching for her or the pillow, never trying to pull it away. It is his body's reflex response to the lack of air. It will be over soon. Soon,

soon. On and on. Down, harder… until… she is gasping for breath, too. Until her arms begin to falter beneath her. Until…

At last.

This is what Grace sees.

At last.

At last, it was done. He was dead. Dead in the heart of winter, when half the country was dying, of pneumonia, bronchitis, influenza, tuberculosis, let alone those whose lungs had been reduced to scraps of wheezing offal by the gas. The doctor came and went, signing a piece of paper, questioning nothing but *my* health, *my* well-being. Another fool.

'He is at rest, at last,' I murmured, eyes suitably moist and lowered. 'He is free.'

Meaning: 'I am free.'

But not then. He would not even leave me, then. The ground was frozen, there was a backing up of burials. He would have to stay in the house for a week or more. Besides, it appeared that this was the way of the Welsh, to make the most of any passing, and it seemed that Edmund Bligh was well-thought of in the community. Weak, foolish Edmund was well-liked. Something I had never known.

They came then, every day, most of whom I had never seen before, men with their hats in their hands, and words that stuck in their throats. Women with hats on their heads and words and words and words pouring out, swamping me in tea and sympathy – those I could understand. Some I knew, recognising them from the women in the Square, come to see what they could see, hear what they could hear, searching for confirmation of what they were sure they knew – that Mrs Edmund Bligh cared nothing for her dead husband.

Well, they did not get it then, nor later by the graveside, when he was buried, finally, beside his parents and son, and all the other Blighs. I stood there, sniffing into my handkerchief. No, I did not rend my garments, or tear at my hair, or make to fling myself into the grave along with him, knowing that such a display of amateur theatricals would count against me, rather than for, would add to their suspicion and cries of hypocrisy. No, just a bowed head, a few tears, a trembling, and a desire to stand by the grave, alone, after the service, after all the other mourners had shuffled down the steep path, to their waiting cars and carts. Then I lifted the veil back from my face, and I looked up from the earth, and across to where the entire village lay, and whereas before I had felt condemned to be trapped within it for all eternity, now I laughed.

'Goodbye,' I whispered, not to my dead husband, but to his body-scourging, thought-blighting, spirit-daunting dwelling place: home.

Gone, I would soon be gone. All I needed to do was sell the house, take the money, and leave. London, I thought. 'I will go back to London.' Paris, even! Why not? Or the south of France, to the sun… oh yes, the sun.

Rumour… words said in a different way. No more than a Chinese whisper, borne on the wind from one person to the next, on a loose sheet of newsprint caught on the breeze. Rumours had reached even this back of beyond of the new life lived in the cities, where flappers danced in short hair and short skirts, while champagne and diamonds flowed. But now there was new talk. Talk of factories and mines closing, jobs disappearing, banks failing.

'Wait till the Spring,' the agent told me. 'There is always more interest in the Spring.' Then, with April gone, 'Summer,' he said, 'maybe it will be better when the weather improves.'

But, of course, it never improved, it was never any better. And suddenly, it was winter again, perpetual twilight again.

Another winter to be spent, bleak and marrow-numbed. Worse, the bank would no longer lend me money against the sale of the house, and the allowance from Edmund's father must help to pay what I already owed.

'Sell something,' the manager suggested.

'There is nothing to sell,' I replied.

'The books,' he said. 'Mr. Bligh's collection. Even in these troubled times, you will find buyers for those. Such volumes are valuable beyond reckoning – in pristine condition, of course… as I know Edmund's to be.'

Oh, my agony, then! What had I done? What had I been? A greater fool than any.

'Surely you can lend some small amount?' I tried. But it seemed that the bank itself had no money. Nor the country, the world, even – the world that I thought lay before me dwindled down to a kitchen, and the bedroom above it, rooms heated with broken chair-legs and lit by fretful candle-light, echoing with nothing but silence.

And then…

And then… a sound. A step, a clang, a flutter. Not so strange – the sound of the brass letter-box. Not so strange – the sight of a cream vellum envelope on the mat. Letters still came for Edmund now and then, whilst bills came for me, wrapped in thin, white paper. I threw all into the stove straight away.

I picked it up. I turned it over, and there it was. 'Mrs Esther Bligh'. I opened it; so it began.

'Dear Esther Bligh,'

So beautifully written, such enticing letters… Curved, and flowing, perfectly aligned, sweet to begin with, drawing me in.

'I trust this finds you well... so much you have been through... your son dead, and then your husband... Sad, so sad...'

Plump Ssses sweeping up and round, so sinuous; 'e' curling in and over, the nib shading. 'Esther' written every few lines, as if I were being talked to. As if we were friends.

Then: whore, bitch, slut, harlot, Jezebel, Lot's wife, she-devil, snake, trollop, vixen. No, not all at once, it's true. But enough.

Still, what was that but name-calling? I had endured worse. Sticks and bleedin' stones again. I knew already there was no signature, but it was surely just one of those hags in the village, venting her spleen, saying now what they had always wanted to say, or did say, when I passed them in the Square. Did they think I wouldn't understand, simply because they talked in a foreign tongue? I knew by their beading eyes, their twisted mouths. They would have spat, if that were something God-fearing women were allowed to do. They may as well have spat. Oh such scorn, in their up-and-down gaze. Oh, how they hated me. Me... 'her', 'that woman' – they never gave me a name. It was so easy to imagine their conversations, behind their claws, behind their nets, when they gathered in their coven. 'I said it from the moment I first set eyes on her.' 'Trouble, I said.' 'He's going to regret this.' 'It will only end badly.' 'Surely just after his money.' 'Poor man. Poor Edmund. Poor Mr Bligh.'

What did they see in me that made them think these things? What was it about me, that made them think of evil? That I had come from away? That I wore lipstick in too bright a colour? That I had stockings and high-heel shoes? That I wore bright clothes – red, oh, sin of sins! – instead of their greys, blacks and browns?

Now here was one of them, getting her revenge. That was all.

It was nothing, until… 'I know what you have done.'

Until… 'murderer'.

Another letter, and another and another.

Words coming at me, as hard as sticks and stones.

Hard black lines, soft black curves, hitting, twisting, flailing my flesh.

On and on and on.

No, no they cannot know, there is no way, there can be no proof.

Who? The doctor. Perhaps the doctor. But the doctor was dead himself.

The lumpen maid? But she had been gone by that time. Besides, she could hardly spew two words between her lips, let alone put pen to paper.

Such a skilled pen, with its copper-plate precision and its curlicues and flourishes, with its perfect English, in spelling and grammar. Not the hand of any of the born-and-bred imbeciles, surely. But if not them, who?

Harlot, Jezebel, Lot's wife. Words I had heard before.

Black-wrought script I had seen before, on the inside of a bible, that I had scribbled over, gouged through, and thrown into the flames. Maud Elizabeth Bligh, married to Arthur, mother of Edmund Bligh. Had she seen what I had done? Was she still here now, or had she returned to torment me? Or was it sent from the spirit world, written in a spirit hand?

Foolish thoughts, all. Nonsense. For I did not believe in ghosts.

Black letters, fine and small, like flies, that I tried to swat away from my head, but still they came, nagging, itching, biting.

Red letters, huge, misshapen.

Precise black lines, on heavy cream sheets.

Crude red daubs, on grey stone. Only two words. Only two could fit between the window and door – or almost. Whore! Murd— Enough. Letters that dripped, blood that dripped. They left the body of the pig on the front lawn.

A man – only a man could do such a thing, though, no doubt, following the instruction of a woman.

Words I could not put on the fire, except I had not put the others on the fire.

I scrubbed with bleach, till my hands were raw, until they became ghost words – faint wraiths of what had been real.

Back-to-front letters, inside-out words, scrawled in the misted windows. Clear lines and curves in frosted grey, dripping water, now, not blood. Tears falling from them, as I puzzled their meaning, whilst knowing what they said, what they were calling me.

What, who, who, what?

What did they know, how could they know, who, who, who?

I would wait till dusk, before going out, then. If I had to go out. I would wear my black widow's clothes, and walk in the shadows, and wait till I saw the shop empty, before going in. Sometimes, I could not avoid people, and I would look at them looking at me, and wonder. Who? Is it you, or you, or you? The old women would cross the road, and mothers would gather their children to them, and the children would gurn and gibber, and the post-mistress would turn away.

She knows, I would think, she of all would know. She, and the postman, knowing the hand-writing of every resident.

Or… is it her? Knowing everything that goes on in this place. Does she know *that*? Is she the one?

Food could be delivered, she told me, now. It was plain she did not want me in her shop, and neither did I want to go there again. I did not want to go anywhere. Except…

home.

It is dark in Esther's house now. It *is* Esther's house, it has been, all along. She is still here, after all.

Here she is, scuttling crab-like between kitchen and bedroom, sideways through the shadows cast by the walls, black in black, bent away from the windows, the doors, the world outside. Lighting the fire to warm her meal, herself, only at night, so that 'they' cannot watch, they cannot know what she does.

A stone, one night. A handful of pebbles, the next. The gibbering voices rising to where she lies. That is when she opens the door of her old room at the back of the house, and now, she likes what she sees. This is where she will sleep, now. This is where she will spend her days, taking her food there – bread, and cheese, perhaps. She eats little else now. Sometimes, she forgets to eat at all. There seems no reason for it.

She sees no reason for it – the woman who catches sight of someone else as she passes the mirror in the hall. A woman in black, with a white-powdered face, who keeps her head down and her eyes low.

'Who are you?' she asks, in a voice she does not recognise, a voice that scuffs her lips as she speaks, then scours the air. Then she laughs, a bark in her throat, and moves on.

'Bitch, fucking bitch, bastards all. Whore, bitch, liar, thief they call me. Who do they fucking think they are?'

No, no, no. She clasps her hands to her ears. She hates the words, who is saying them? Where is she? Where is this person with the sewer-pipe mouth? She looks for her behind the curtains, in the cupboard. There is no-one there, but still the words go on, and on, and on. Not the written words of the letters any more, though they are still all around, plaguing her, as usual, never letting her rest. Not the spoken words of the children. Not the voices returned, and turned against her, or new voices come. Someone is speaking, someone so close to her, someone—

'You, you fucking stupid bitch! You!'

She doesn't go out. But the day comes when she has used every tin in the cupboard and she has no choice but to go. She will wear the black, and walk in the dusk, with head and eyes down, but still she sees them looking at her. Well, it is what they have always done. There, here, before, now. But now… the looks, the noises they make are different. The older children cross to the other side of the street, the mothers push the younger ones behind them, then hurry them away. She knows all this, though she doesn't see; but she smells it. She knows that it is fear. But what has *she* done? Nothing, she has done nothing! Or… did she?

And yet, here is Mrs Evans… coming from behind the counter, to put a hand on her arm, and say 'Are you all right, bach?' until a snarl snaps her back into her place, muttering and shaking her head.

Grace will not go out any more, she will have her food brought to her in a box left outside the door. That is what she will do. That is what she does, spending most of her days, her nights, in the small room, lying on her bed, trying to hear the beat of her heart between the words, wondering when it will stop.

– Burn them. I will burn them, like I did with the first… Did I? Like I should have done with all of them. Burn them without opening them. Like you should have done. They weren't addressed to you. They were my letters. How dare you open my personal mail? How dare you learn my secrets and spread them around? You bitch. Did I? Did you?

Look at them, a cairn of cream pulp and white tissue, veined black, blocking the way to the door. Immovable, unless a strong gust from outside or my step shudders through them and sends the latest arrival tumbling down. I will pick them up in handfuls and carry them to the stove and put an end to them once and for all. Use them for fuel, like the postman told you a life-time ago. Sit there, warming yourself on them, making good from them, laughing at whoever penned them.

No, no, no. Burn them where they lie. Get a match – or a taper, a taper would be better, knowing how fickle matches can be, how they can let you down. Bring a taper, and push it into the middle of them, at the bottom where the straw rush of the mat will add extra fuel, where the draught beneath the door will blow onto the flames: and the flames will somersault on the scattered paper, across the mat to the stairs. The dry, old, wood-worm eaten stairs, until—

Yes, I will fetch the taper, and I will sit for a while on the bottom step and watch as my curse takes hold. I didn't watch before.

Before, the first time I did this, I ran. A shame. I wanted to stay and look, to make sure, and to see it. To see the house I had been born in, had grown up in, lost in flame and smoke. To see the rats run out, the grins wiped off their faces, to savour the stench of smoke instead of stew and piss. It wouldn't have taken long – it was no more than a wooden shack, after all, with rooms of cloth, and furniture from sticks. With no-one inside it… no, no-one inside it. You made sure, I made sure. Sure that my mother, and my brother, and my two younger sisters were at the market that day – and your father, who had come home so drunk the night before, so that you knew as soon as he came in what was going to happen, as it always happened, but— He always left early, didn't he? No matter how drunk. Didn't he? He wouldn't have still been lying on my bed, would he, exhausted and finished after what he had done? No, no, no. It was only the house I wanted to destroy, to see go up in flames, only I didn't… I ran…

But I will see this now, you have to see, it is good to see. It is good to see fire, when you have always loved fire, since that first day, knowing it for what it can do. Knowing it for its colour, its reds, its blues, its purple, even, the most surprising colour. Look, there! See! The purple heart wrapped in gold. The golden frittered edge of that paper crown. See! See how it skips across to the ragged rug, catching its frayed strands, stretching out towards you, to welcome you.

No, no, no. Better to go to my room, better to shut myself in there, and lie down on my hard, narrow bed. It is safe there, or safer than anywhere here. I will be safe. I will check the clasp on the shutters, pull the curtains, shut the door tight, like I always do. I will get into bed, and draw the quilt over my head, and…

Yes. And yes, I am warm here, warmer than I have ever been before. Already, I can feel the heat below getting stronger, reaching up towards me. The words are being burnt away, the words are being replaced by heat. The words are finally being destroyed. Good, good, good. Now something else slinks under the door – not words, good, good, not words, no – but smoke. Grey, winding, like the words used to be, sly, curling, like the words, but it is just smoke, only smoke. It won't hurt me, like the words hurt me. I will have peace now. At last.

But… Words. Louder than ever, coming at me, shouting at me, louder than they have ever done before. Noise. Banging, clanging, barging through the walls, the quilt, my hands that are clutched to my ears. A name. Whose name? Or just a word… Grace.

Grace. GRACE.

On, and on, and on. A hammer is knocking at my skull. A saw is splintering my eyes apart. A shout is exploding in my ears. More words, more and more. They are coming for me. They are breaking into my safe little room; they are tearing down the door, they are smashing through the window, they are… The fire hasn't finished them, after all. They have fed off its heat, and they are here. Now. NOW.

It is quiet again now, so peaceful as she sits in the window of the flat above the post-office, and watches the sea. It is such a beautiful day! The sky is blue, the water is blue, and laps gently towards the front. The scene directly before her looks just like a picture postcard. But the town that stretches away from her on either side has changed. She had been foolish to think it could be the same, after two world wars, and the hardship of the years between. And its location beneath the mountains means the railway will never come here. It will never be the holiday destination she imagined, she remembered from her honeymoon. Perhaps it never was. But still, on a fine day…

Beneath her, the old women gather for their daily chat, look up, and, seeing her, smile and wave. Mrs. Jones, Mrs. Davies, Mrs. Monaghan. She knows their names now. They introduced themselves when they brought her 'hand-me-downs' and 'cast-aways' from their worldly goods, 'to help'; 'so that you will not be without, love'; 'so you've got something!' How could she ever have thought they were cold and unkind? How she wished she had let people help her after John's death. Perhaps, then, none of this would have happened. And their voices… she loves the up and down lilt of their words; she could listen to them all day. She smiles down at them, and waves back.

There is a knock at the door.

'Can I get you anything, bach?' Mrs Evans asks her. She is staying with the Evanses 'for as long as you want, bach, as long as you need.'

'No, thank you, I'm fine. You are so kind. Everybody is so kind.'

'Oh, it's nothing, love. Dim ots. Nothing at all. Just you shout when you want your tea.'

It was Mrs. Evans's son who pulled her from her bed, through the back window. Just in time, they said. As soon as they'd seen the smoke, half the men of the village had rushed to the house, and worked to put out the fire, and reach and rescue her. She'd been lucky, very lucky. Thank goodness she had unfastened the shutters in time. Thank goodness she had woken.

She didn't tell them how John had shouted to her, shouted and shouted until she had to listen; how, otherwise, she would have just carried on lying there, until—

There are lots of other things she hasn't told them, just as she is sure they keep plenty to themselves. But she knows, now, about a recent spate of poison-pen letters in the village, how several people had been victims of the vicious attacks. The local policeman had dealt with it… Sergeant Thomas. He had come to explain it to her. 'It's something that happens in a small place from time to time. Gossip getting out of hand, and put down on paper. A bad show.' He had told her how, as a constable, some twenty years ago, he had found Esther Bligh dead in her bed – the same bed Grace had been sleeping in.

'From starvation, they reckoned. Nobody had seen her for months. And nobody had cared to go and look.'

That answered… something, she supposed – the new letters, and… As for the rest…

John has gone now for good, she is sure, and all the other voices – *all.* When she leaves, to go back… somewhere, she will be on her own, she will have to start again, somehow, because, of course, the house had been burnt to the ground, along with everything in it.

She is glad. It means there is nothing left of Esther any more. There is nothing left of the words any more. There is nothing left of that other. She will be only 'her'.

It is light again. Good. I have got the light back now.

I have got light, and colour and air – everything that had been taken from me.

I can breathe! I can glide down the street, so fast that no-one seems to feel me, beyond a lift in their hair, a brush against their coats.

The noises I hear are sounds I want to hear – hustle and bustle, and music and idle chatter. Some, it is true, are different from those I was used to, just as the world is a different place, for time has moved on. I have moved on.

On from the dark, on from that house, from that place, back to the city where I belong. To streets, with shops and theatres and public houses, things I can understand, the crowds who speak in a language I understand. A shame, then, that they don't understand me, or hear, or see, or touch me. I am nothing to them, beyond that shiver, that frown, that question.

Still—

Still, the words are gone. They have left me, or I have left them – left them in the ashes of that house, black lost in black, burned as they should have been from the start.

No more whore and bitch and slut, unless I choose to move amongst the alley-ways and red lights, except I don't.

No more Jezebel, and harlot, and Lot's wife, unless I should find myself in a church on a Sunday morning, but, of course, I stay away.

I stay away from all those things. I go, just where I want to go.

I am me, again. Esther Thorpe, dancing in a dress of rainbow colours, with lips of shining scarlet, and diamonds, rubies, emeralds decked upon her.

Mrs Edmund Bligh, Mrs Esther Bligh, Esther Bligh – she is gone. Gone for good.

Now there is only Grace.

Acknowledgements

Thanks to Helen Carey and Maria Donovan, two authors who helped me believe I could write.

To my writing group, for all their encouragement and support… and great company!

To Robert Peett, for making this happen.

A different kind of gratitude to my wonderful family and friends, who are always there for me – especially, of course, to the boys and their loved ones. I am so lucky to have you.

And to Dai, most of all, for putting up with my dreaming.

About The Author

Diana Powell was born and brought up in Llanelli, South Wales, and studied English at Aberystwyth University. Her short stories have featured in a number of competitions. She won the 2014 PENfro prize, and in 2016 was long-listed for the Sean O'Faolain, short-listed for the Over the Edge New Writer, and was a runner-up in the Cinnamon Press awards. Her work has been published in several journals and anthologies.

'Esther Bligh' is her first novella.

She now lives with her husband in beautiful Pembrokeshire, and is currently working on a collection of stories, and a new novel.